"I have a proposition for you."

Amelia's eyes widened, her lips parting farther as she whooshed out a deep breath. "Go on," she prompted, though it sounded as if she'd rather do just about anything else than hear whatever was coming next.

"Come with us."

She blinked, shaking her head a little. "What do you mean?"

"At the end of the school year, I will take Cameron to my island to live. Come with him, and help him to adjust to his new life. Help him adjust to me." The final request surprised Santos; he hadn't planned on admitting how hard he was finding it to bond with his son, nor to forgive Cynthia for keeping their child a secret. Whenever he looked at Cameron he could see only what he'd missed out on, not what he'd gained.

"You're asking me to go to Agrios Nisi with you?"

Clare Connelly was raised in small-town Australia among a family of avid readers. She spent much of her childhood up a tree, Harlequin book in hand. Clare is married to her own real-life hero, and they live in a bungalow near the sea with their two children. She is frequently found staring into space—a surefire sign she is in the world of her characters. She has a penchant for French food and ice-cold champagne, and Harlequin novels continue to be her favorite-ever books. Writing for Harlequin Presents is a long-held dream. Clare can be contacted via clareconnelly.com or on her Facebook page.

Books by Clare Connelly

Harlequin Presents

Bought for the Billionaire's Revenge
Innocent in the Billionaire's Bed
Her Wedding Night Surrender
Bound by the Billionaire's Vows
Spaniard's Baby of Revenge
Redemption of the Untamed Italian
The Secret Kept from the King

Secret Heirs of Billionaires

Shock Heir for the King

Christmas Seductions

Bound by Their Christmas Baby
The Season to Sin

Crazy Rich Greek Weddings

The Greek's Billion-Dollar Baby
Bride Behind the Billion-Dollar Veil

Visit the Author Profile page
at Harlequin.com for more titles.

Clare Connelly

———

HIRED BY THE IMPOSSIBLE GREEK

HARLEQUIN®
PRESENTS®

Recycling programs
for this product may
not exist in your area.

ISBN-13: 978-1-335-14868-1

Hired by the Impossible Greek

Copyright © 2020 by Clare Connelly

Harlequin Enterprises ULC
22 Adelaide St. West, 40th Floor
Toronto, Ontario M5H 4E3, Canada
www.Harlequin.com

Printed in U.S.A.

HIRED BY THE
IMPOSSIBLE GREEK

PROLOGUE

IT WAS THE fourth time he'd been called upon to act in this capacity at one of these events, but undoubtedly not the last. For each of the previous four weddings, Santos Anastakos had been required to stand dutifully at his father Nico's side—best man, oldest son, quietly watchful—as his father had promised yet another woman to love her for as long as they both should live.

Santos's expression as he surveyed the guests was unknowingly cynical. Despite the alleged joy of the occasion, Santos couldn't summon much more than a vague degree of tolerance for his father's proclivities. Proclivities that had seen him marry eight—nine, counting today—women over the span of his lifetime.

It's different this time, Santos. This time, she's 'the one'.

Santos had long since given up arguing with his father about the foolishness of his marriage addiction. Similarly he'd abandoned firm suggestions that Nico get counselling for what had become an embarrassing and ridiculous tendency to fall in love faster than most people changed jobs.

All Santos could do was watch from the side lines

and quarantine the Anastakos fortune from any fallout from the inevitable divorce. It was ungenerous to entertain such thoughts whilst standing at the front of a crowded, ancient church, listening to Nico and his latest bride proclaim their 'love' for one another.

How could that concept fail to earn his derision when he'd seen, over and over and over again, how quickly and completely love turned to hate and hurt? His own mother had been overthrown for the next Mrs Anastakos when Santos had been only three years old, and Santos had been shuttled between father and mother for the next few years before—at his father's insistence—being sent off to boarding school.

As the chaplain joyously proclaimed the happy—for now, at least—couple man and wife, Santos grimaced. He had made himself a promise after his father's third marriage had dissolved in a particularly bitter and public fashion: he would never be foolish enough to get married, nor to fall 'in love', whatever the hell that meant—and nothing in his thirty-four years had tempted Santos to question that resolve. Marriage was for fools and hopeless romantics—of which, he was proud to say, he was neither.

CHAPTER ONE

Three months later

'YES?' THE SINGLE word was infused with derision, impatience and a Greek accent that, while she'd known to expect it, still caught Amelia a little off-guard. She stared at the man—Santos Anastakos—for several seconds, the purpose for coming to this grand estate in the English countryside momentarily forgotten as she computed several things at lightning speed.

There was something so vibrant and charismatic about the man—so larger than life, so glowering and intimidating—that she could only stare at him, blinking for several seconds, as she scrambled her brain back into working order. He was dressed in a tuxedo, styled for an evening somewhere considerably grander than even this beautiful, ancient country home.

'Mr Anastakos?' she confirmed, though of course it was him—she'd seen his photograph in the papers around the time of Cameron's mother's death, when news had broken that the billionaire magnate had fathered a love child over six years earlier.

'Yes?' The word was again impatient. A light breeze

rustled past, giving a hint of relief on this summer's evening, and her long, dark hair shifted a little, an errant clutch pushing across her face so she had to lift a hand to contain it, instinctively brushing it away and tucking it behind her ear.

'Darling, we're going to have to get a move on if we're to make it on time.' A woman's voice came from within the house, echoing across the marbled tiles which glittered and shone beneath Santos's handcrafted shoes.

'I don't have all night,' he expelled, his lips flattening into a frown. 'Are you lost? Did your car break down?' His eyes were wide-set and almond-shaped and lined by thick, dark lashes. Where his complexion was swarthy and dark, his eyes were the most magnificent blue, almost silver, with flecks of black close to the iris. They shifted beyond her now, as if searching for a car or some other physical clue as to why she was here.

'Not at all. I came here to speak with you.'

His eyes narrowed, returning to her face, and she wished quite illogically that they'd turn away once more. There was something in the strength of his gaze that caused her usually unflappable pulse to flutter in a way that was incredibly unsettling. It increased when his gaze travelled downward, over the plain pink blouse she wore, towards the cream trousers that were shaped over her slender hips and legs. It was little more than a cursory inspection, as though her outfit might give away some hint of who she was and what she was doing on his doorstep.

'Have we met before?' There was a hint of wariness in his question, an emotion she couldn't fathom.

'No, sir. Not at all.'

Relief. She frowned, wondering how many people he must meet to think he'd forgotten her. 'Then what can I do for you?'

'I'm Amelia Ashford…'

'Ashford.' She could see the moment comprehension dawned. 'The famous Miss Ashford?'

'I don't know about that.' She smiled even when the idea of fame had her wanting to curl up in a ball and hide. Fame was the reason she'd opted to use her grandmother's surname when taking up this teaching position—a desire to be known only for her teaching work and nothing else.

'You are Cameron's teacher?'

'Yes.' She smiled at him, a crisp smile that flashed on her face like lightning then disappeared again. 'I wanted to speak to you about your son.'

His shoulders squared at that, as though he resented her description of their relationship. But that wasn't Amelia's concern, whatever the rumours said—and there were plenty, about this man's parental neglect of Cameron, his refusal to support Cameron's mother… It wasn't for Amelia to speculate. Her only care was the little boy of whom she'd always been fond and whom she now considered to be quite dear to her. Perhaps her estrangement from her own parents made her feel more invested in Cameron than she otherwise would have been…but, no. The little boy was special and the grief he was suffering through demanded advocacy and support.

'Is something the matter?'

She compressed her lips, trying not to express any

overt hostility. So far as she knew, this man had very little experience with children in general and his son in particular. Perhaps he didn't realise how unusual an occurrence it was for a primary schoolteacher to arrive at a parent's doorstep at eight o'clock in the evening.

It was unusual, but Amelia had timed it thus on purpose in the hope of avoiding Cameron. She hadn't wanted her little pupil to overhear them, nor to know more than he needed to at this point.

'This conversation would be better had inside. May I come in?'

His brows drew together, thick and full, giving his expression a forbidding and darkly handsome look. She thought then how intimidating he might be to some people, those who had to work with him or relied on his good opinion in order to advance professionally. Fortunately for Amelia, neither of those things applied to her. She was able to be professional and confident, her motives for coming to him motivated purely by concern for her young pupil.

'Do you make a habit of turning up uninvited at the homes of your students?'

'Not at all, sir, which should give you some clue as to how important I consider this matter to be.'

'What exactly do you consider to be important?'

'Your son.'

Again, there was something in his features, a look of annoyance or frustration, but it was gone again almost immediately. 'The nanny has put Cameron to bed already. If you wanted to see him...'

Her heart squeezed at that, and she swept her eyes shut for a moment, forcefully pushing emotions to the side. But, oh, it was almost impossible when she remembered Cynthia McDowell, who had adored and doted on her son, who had made up for all the lack of money in the world with an abundance of love and interest. To think of the dear little boy losing his mother, inheriting this man as a father and being shunted into a nanny's care all in the space of less than two months!

It only galvanised her, making her feel even more strongly about her reasons for coming to Renway Hall so late on a Friday evening. 'It's you I'd like to speak to, Mr Anastakos.'

'And it can't wait until Monday?'

She considered that a moment. 'Would Monday suit you better?'

'Not necessarily.' He shifted his shoulders. 'I'm not sure if any time would be convenient, given that I have no idea what you've come to discuss.'

'You'll just have to take it on trust, then, that I wouldn't be here if it weren't important.'

'I don't take anyone on trust,' he asserted silkily, nonetheless taking a step backward and gesturing into the hall. 'But I am intrigued.' He cast a glance at his wristwatch. 'I have five minutes.'

She bristled at that and—barely—resisted an inclination to point out that discussing his son's emotional health and welfare was something for which he should prioritise a little more time, particularly in the wake of recent events, but she didn't. It was important to keep her mind on what she wanted, and arguing unnecessarily with this man would do nothing to achieve her goal.

'Come with me.' He turned, walking down the corridor. She had a brief impression of an endless expanse of tiles and walls lined with ancient art—one in particular caught her eye, so she stopped walking for a moment to look at it properly.

'This is a Camareli.'

She felt him stop and turn without even looking in his direction. There was something about his presence that seemed to puncture the air around her—it wasn't necessary to look at him to know how he moved. He was dynamic, as though his absolute magnitude was so bright it was almost overpowering.

The painting depicted a Madonna scene. Bright colours had been used, but it was the nature of the brush strokes that had revealed the artist's hand before Amelia had seen the small signature in the bottom-right-hand corner of the painting.

'Yes.' And then, after a moment's silence, 'But we're not here to discuss art, are we, Miss Ashford?'

She jerked her gaze to his face, wondering at the rapid hammering of her pulse, the flipping of her heart inside her chest. Her features were cool, her eyes giving away nothing of her internal responses. 'No, Mr Anastakos. We're not.'

He began to move once more, turning through two wide doors into a room that had leather furniture and a grand piano. The art on the walls in here was world-class too—more famous, by artists of greater renown than Camareli. Then again, she'd always had a thing for the lesser known Renaissance painters, and Camareli was just that.

'Maria, Cameron's teacher is here. I'll be a few minutes.'

A stunning blonde woman dressed in a slinky red

gown moved with all the grace of a ballerina, standing from the white leather lounge she'd occupied a moment earlier and subjecting Amelia to the same slow inspection Santos had performed earlier. But, where Santos's eyes had seemed to trail heat over Amelia's body, the other woman's left only ice in their wake.

'But, darling, we'll be late,' Maria pouted.

Santos expelled a breath so his nostrils flared and his features showed disdain. 'Apparently it can't wait. Call Leo—he'll make you a cocktail.'

'Oh, fine, but if I'd known this would involve baby sitting and being abandoned all night I would never have come,' Maria complained, turning her slender body away from Santos and Amelia.

Amelia, for her part, could only look at Maria with a sense of wonder—she'd never seen a woman in the flesh who was so like some kind of Hollywood celebrity. Everything about her was a study in perfection, from her figure to her sheening hair; from her flawless make-up and sky-high heels to manicured nails.

'She's very beautiful,' Amelia remarked conversationally as they left the room, returning to the long marbled corridor.

'Yes,' Santos returned in almost the same tone, pausing at another doorway. This time, it led to an office, all modern furniture and computers. There was more artwork here, and a large mirror that showed a reflection of the stables.

He closed the door behind them and Amelia—for no reason she could think of—jumped a little.

'So, Miss Ashford? You have my full attention; what would you like to speak to me about?'

He gestured to one of the seats opposite his desk. She took it, crossing her legs and placing her hands in her lap, her eyes following him across the room, where he paused at a bar and opened a crystal Scotch decanter. He poured two generous measures then handed a glass to her, their fingertips brushing as he placed the Scotch in the palm of her hand.

'Thank you.' She cradled the Scotch without taking a sip. She'd bypassed the usual phases of wild abandon and teenage letting down of hair and had never really developed a tolerance for or interest in alcohol. Every now and again she enjoyed a few sips of a nice wine with a special dinner, or champagne on Christmas Eve, but it certainly wasn't something she imbibed on a daily basis.

Unlike Santos, she gathered, as he threw half of his own Scotch back in one go before resting his bottom on the edge of his desk, rather than taking up the seat opposite, so he was much closer to her than she'd anticipated. His long legs were just to her right, so she could reach out and touch them if she wanted.

The thought threw her completely off-balance in a way she'd never experienced in her life. She'd been on a few dates, but they had been academic exercises more than anything, something she'd been encouraged to try at Brent's urging and never really found comfortable or fun.

You have to give it time, Millie. Get to know a guy, see his good side. Just go with the flow!

But those dates had all ended the same way—with Amelia feeling bored out of her brain and wanting nothing more than never to see the man again. One particular date had left her so bored she'd almost fallen asleep at the table. It was very rare for her to factor her intellect into her thoughts but, at times like that, it was impossible not to realise that being a child genius, being exposed to some of the world's greatest minds from a very young age, had left her with absolutely zero tolerance for small talk. And particularly not with men who were quite clearly preoccupied with the more physical aspects of the evening.

A shudder shifted through her at the whole failed debacle of dating, but that didn't explain why now, so close to Santos Anastakos, she felt heat building inside her blood, warming her from the inside out.

The sooner she could get this over and done with, the better. She had to plead Cameron's case and then leave—she never had to see Santos again after that.

She geared herself up to start speaking, to say what she'd come to say, but Santos spoke first, his eyes roaming her face quite freely, his gaze curious now, speculative in a way that did nothing to help her overheating blood.

'How old are you?'

'I beg your pardon?'

His expression shifted; for a moment she saw scepticism there, perhaps even disapproval. 'You look too young to be a teacher.'

She ran her finger around the edge of the Scotch glass, feeling the indents in its shape. 'I've been at Elesmore for a little over three years.'

She brushed aside his disbelief. It wasn't necessary to tell him that she'd graduated with her first degree—physics—at the age of eleven, completed her second degree by thirteen and a postgraduate doctorate by fifteen, before doing an about-turn and deciding she wanted to become a teacher. He didn't need to know that she'd graduated from her education degree at sixteen and had spent a few years travelling and consulting for various space agencies before finally accepting a position in a small local comprehensive on the basis they wouldn't advertise who she was.

Anonymity and a lack of pressure had been her goal—normality after a lifetime of being pushed through one hoop to another.

'Which makes you…?' he prompted, taking another sip of his Scotch. His throat shifted as he swallowed and she found her gaze focussed on his skin there, covered by a hint of stubble, dark and thick. It would feel bristly if she reached up and ran her fingers across it.

She startled at the thought and wrenched her eyes to the view of the stables just visible in the mirror.

'My age isn't relevant,' she murmured, her fingers tightly gripping the Scotch glass. She was nervous! Amelia hadn't expected that but sitting in this man's office now, surrounded by proof of his business acumen and success, it was impossible not to recognise how dynamic and powerful he was—imposingly so. That was why she felt as though a kaleidoscope of butterflies had been let loose in her belly.

'Fine, then, let's discuss what is relevant,' he responded with a hint of something in his voice— something cold and unwelcoming, as though she were wasting his time and he wanted her gone.

'Mr Larcombe told me you're planning to pull Cameron out of Elesmore. That not only are you looking to remove him from the school he's been at since he was three years old, you're also intending to move him to Greece once the term ends.'

Silence fell, a silence that was thick and unpleasant, but Amelia resolutely didn't interrupt it, and several beats passed, each heavy with the words she'd flung at him; each filled with nothing but the sound of her thudding heart.

'And...?' The word was drawled by his lips, lips that were wide and chiselled, harsh and compelling; lips that drew her attention far more than she was comfortable with.

'And? Is it true?'

'Do you imagine the school headmaster lied to you?' His question was teasing, gently sarcastic in nature. It wasn't intended to be rude, she thought, but that didn't stop it from having an immediate effect on her.

Heat began to bloom in her cheeks. She wasn't used to being treated like an imbecile. She glared at him forcefully, her expression clearly showing how unimpressed she was, but she forced a brittle smile into place, remembering the old adage that you caught more bees with honey. 'I hoped he'd made a mistake somehow.'

'He didn't.' Santos shifted a little, inadvertently brushing her knee with his. It was like being jolted with a thousand volts of electricity. She stared at him in surprise, a reaction she was nowhere near experienced enough to conceal, and saw speculation move over his features. She blinked her eyes closed, before turning them towards the view once more, but it wasn't quite enough. He'd seen her reaction and was now wondering at the reason for it.

Great.

She was literally the opposite of the sophisticated beauty in the room down the hallway. Where Maria was stunning and expensive-looking, Amelia felt dowdy, dull and quite utterly out of her depth even having a conversation with a man like this. For goodness' sake, his *knee* had touched her knee and she was permitting that to turn her stomach into a tangle of knots! Preposterous.

'When the school year finishes, Cameron will move to Agrios Nisi with me.' He spoke as though he hadn't even realised they'd touched—his bloodstream wasn't running with the force of a thousand wild stallions.

'Why?'

'Because it's where I live. And I am apparently his father.'

She ignored the last remark. 'But what is there for him on Agrios Nisi?' The words were delivered with uncharacteristic fire, but Amelia couldn't help it. Ever since the headmaster had relayed the plans to Amelia, her head had been swimming with disapproval, and her heart with a sense of panic and pain. It wasn't right to drag Cameron away from everything and everyone he knew. The little boy deserved better than that, especially now. She knew, better than anyone, what it was like to be sent from pillar to post—and by your parents!

'Apart from miles of pristine coastline and a chance to have the kind of childhood any boy would kill for?'

A small noise of ridicule escaped her lips before she could stop it. 'What he needs, Mr Anastakos, is to be *here*—especially now.' She drew in a breath, trying to calm her racing heart and pounding pulse without much success. 'He's lost so much already this year. To take him away from the friends who adore him—and the faculty who also adore him,' she finished ineptly, her throat thick with the pain of how much Cameron had come to mean to her, 'Will be to inflict further trauma on a little boy who's already suffered considerably. I understand things weren't necessarily amicable between you and Cynthia but that hardly seems like a reason to punish Cameron. He deserves you to act in his best interests and keeping him here, in England, at Elesmore, is the very least you can do.'

'My relationship with Cameron's mother is none of your business.'

Amelia's eyes narrowed. 'No, but how you treat Cameron is, very much so.'

'As for Cynthia,' he continued, as though she hadn't spoken, 'It was neither amicable or otherwise. The truth of the mater is, we barely knew each other.'

Amelia blinked at this sterile description of the woman with whom he'd made a child and shook her head. 'Be that as it may, you clearly knew each other well enough to become parents, and now you're all Cameron has left. He deserves more than this.'

The silence that fell now was punctuated only by the sound of her own breathing. Santos stared at her from eyes that were almost oceanic in colour, his tanned skin slightly flushed along the hard ridges of his cheekbones. It was a face prone to sternness anyway, all symmetrical and sharp, as though a sculptor had been obliged to turn granite into humanity with only a blade as a tool, leaving no room for nuance and undulation, only harsh edges and finality. But now, like this? There was such obvious anger and rejection on his face that Amelia almost regretted coming here.

Almost, but not quite.

Cameron deserved to have someone fight on his behalf. At six, he was too young to realise how the adults in his life had failed him, but Amelia recognised the behaviours and, while she wouldn't ordinarily think of interfering, this was different. Cameron was different.

She refused to fail him.

CHAPTER TWO

'YOU THINK I'M wrong to take him away?' Santos straightened, drawing himself to his full six-and-a-half feet, looking down on the slight schoolteacher with a sense of rumbling fury. It wasn't entirely her fault. He'd carried this anger for weeks now—since learning that a woman he'd spent two nights with seven years ago had borne him a child and failed to mention even a hint of the boy's existence. He'd been denied any chance to know his own son, any chance to prepare for this, until Cynthia had died and both Cameron and Santos had been thrust well and truly into the deep end.

'Yes.' Her eyes didn't quite meet his. It was a frustrating habit she'd shown ever since he'd drawn the door inward to reveal her on the doorstep. One minute she was the personification of timidity and the next she was burning with passion and wild accusations, practically threatening to call child welfare, or whomever looked after inadequate parents in this country.

At least she wasn't attempting to obfuscate now. 'And you think you have any right coming here to lecture me about the choices I make for my son?'

Her eyes glanced in his direction, landing briefly on

his squared jaw before skittering back to the window. His fingers tingled with an urge to reach for her chin and pull it towards him, to draw her stubborn, runaway gaze to his even when she refused to hold it.

'When they're so obviously contrary to his best interests? Yes, sir, I do.'

A muscle ticked at the base of his jaw; he felt it tapping against his flesh and sought to control his emotions before he spoke. 'He is *my* son. I can do whatever the hell I'd like.'

'Even if that's going to hurt him?' She responded with fierceness now and something leaped inside his chest, interest and curiosity combined in one arrow of emotion.

'His mother's death hurt him,' Santos inserted quietly, the words devoid of emotion. 'His mother's choice to keep him a secret from me hurt him—and me—in untold ways. I am only doing what I would have insisted on six years ago, if Cynthia had bothered to inform me of her pregnancy.'

'I'm not interested in that,' the teacher responded, compressing her lips with a primness he found strangely tantalising. If it was true, she was unlike just about anyone in his life had been since Cameron's existence had been revealed. Everyone wanted to know about his secret child. 'However,' she conceded after a moment, 'I appreciate his pain isn't of your causing.'

'That's generous of you.' He took another sip of his Scotch and placed the cup on the edge of his desk, crossing his arms over his chest and staring down at her distractedly.

'Yet.'

She was the definition of dull. So very English, just like Cynthia had been, with that clipped accent and cool disposition. But, where Cynthia had been strikingly attractive and flirtatious, Amelia Ashford looked as though she'd rather be dragged over hot coals than spend another minute in his office. Except...

Yes, except for when their knees had brushed. She'd startled and made a soft noise, almost a moan, her lips parting and her eyes showing surprise. Was it possible that this woman was far less icy than her surface demeanour might suggest?

'If things had been different, perhaps you would have raised him in Greece, but there's no sense losing ourselves in the hypothetical. Cameron is English. He's lived here all his life, never even travelling abroad. His whole world has changed so much since the accident. He was very close to Cynthia; she adored him and every day without her is a struggle for him.' Emotion coloured the last sentence, the threat of tears obvious in her softly voiced observation. 'Perhaps in time, when the shock has lessened and he knows you better, uprooting him wouldn't be such a monumental ask. But right now? I honestly think you'll worsen his grief tenfold. It's not fair, Mr Anastakos.'

'Fair?' He couldn't help himself. Despite the fact he could see the logic in what she was saying, disbelief fired through him, making him want to contradict her. 'You think having a small child dropped on my lap—a child I had no earthly idea existed six weeks ago—and expecting to know what is right or wrong for him is fair?'

'No,' she conceded quietly. 'Nothing about this situation is fair but you're the only one who can make a difference for Cameron. Right now, he needs all of us to pull together and help him. You can't take him away from everything he knows—everyone who knows him. He deserves better than that.'

'My son is an Anastakos. We have lived and died on Agrios Nisi for generations and he will be no different.'

Fire shifted through her eyes once more. Wide and brown, they landed on him with a strength that surprised him. 'Perhaps, but all I'm asking is that you give him time. What harm could come from leaving things as they are for another year? Let him take some solace from the school friends he's known since nursery, from the parents of his friends who know and adore him, from the teachers who—'

'Yes, care for him,' Santos interrupted, wondering why her impassioned plea was so irritating to him. 'You said that.' He didn't move his body by a degree, staying exactly as he was, his gaze heavy on her face. 'You care for my son?'

A hint of colour shifted beneath her olive complexion. 'I care for all my pupils.'

'And so you do this often, then? Go into their houses and accuse their parents of being selfish and wrong?'

Her cheeks darkened in colour as she stood, her throat moving as she swallowed convulsively. 'I'm sorry if I've offended you in some way.' The words were haughty. 'I would never forgive myself if I didn't ask you to reconsider. Cameron deserves that of me.'

She stood directly opposite him, toe to toe, though she was at least a foot shorter, so her head had to tilt in order for her eyes to meet his. 'He deserves more than this.'

Her words rang with accusation, making a mockery of her earlier apology, and something snaked through him, something born of masculine pride and ancient, primaeval impulses.

Her judgement was tightening around his chest and he felt a desire to unsettle her easy blame, to rail at her accusation and make her understand that this last month and a half had been a type of hell on earth for Santos as well. Having a child? It was something he'd always, always sworn he wouldn't do—a mistake he had never intended to replicate. He had a half-brother who could carry on the family name. Santos was free to remain single and alone, just the way he liked it. Having Cameron foisted upon him out of the blue— the product of a two-night affair with a woman he'd long since almost forgotten about—was like a stick of dynamite exploding in his face.

'Tell me, Amelia Ashford.' He couldn't help the mockery that curled through her name. 'What makes you an authority on this? Do you have children?'

Her cheeks were now the colour of the sky beyond the window, a vibrant peach, her eyes darker than the sun-ripened olives that grew wild over the southern side of Agrios Nisi.

'No.' She opened her mouth, no doubt to add further clarity to this, but Santos wasn't interested. He pressed a finger to her lips, intending only to silence her, but the moment his flesh connected with her mouth some- thing tightened deep in his abdomen, hardening in his groin, insisting on being acknowledged.

Her eyes were saucer-wide, her lips parting on what he presumed to be an involuntary sigh. Her breath was warm as it wrapped around his finger, making it a temptation that was almost impossible to ignore. He wanted to sink his fingertip into her mouth, to see her full, pink lips wrap around it while those huge eyes of hers bored into his.

Christos, what was happening? She was hardly his type and, more than that, she'd arrived in his home purely with the intention of berating and insulting him. Perhaps that was it—the challenge in her words made him want to answer in a completely different way, to pull her body to his and drop his mouth, claiming hers, dominating her and answering her questions and accusations all at once...

'No?' He moved his finger, but didn't drop it away completely. Instead, he drew it sideways, along her cheek, before padding his thumb over her lower lip, cupping the side of her face in his palm and holding her beneath him, forcing her eyes to meet his after all.

She swallowed hard; he felt the movement of her jaw. 'I don't have children. But I do know Cameron.'

The words were husky and thick, desire making them more stilted than her previous verbal lashings.

His lips twisted in silent acknowledgement of that; he was no longer interested in discussing his surprise love child with this woman. He moved his body forward almost imperceptibly, closing the small distance between them just sufficiently to feel the softness of her surprisingly generous breasts against his chest.

'I—'

'Yes, Amelia?' What the hell was he doing? Playing

with fire, that was what. She was his son's teacher and she'd come to him with perfectly legitimate concerns. While Santos Anastakos might have earned himself the moniker of billionaire playboy in the tabloids and on gossip blogs, he always knew where to draw the line. He'd never once become involved with a member of his staff, nor had he become involved in affairs—he didn't do messy, complicated, emotional. This woman didn't exactly work for him but nor was this straightforward. She'd come to him with concerns about his son and he was turning that into a sensual game of cat and mouse, enjoying the way she was sparring with him even when he resented the hell out of her accusations. This wasn't a date; it wasn't just a random encounter in a hotel bar. She was his child's schoolteacher, so why was he suddenly overcome with an urge to make love to her, right here and now?

Hell, he had Maria waiting for him in the other room, and there was very little doubt in Santos's mind as to how she wanted their evening together to end. If he wanted sex, then it was there at his disposal, but this wasn't about the slaking of a physical need. There was something about this particular woman that was drawing him in, making him want her with an urgency he hadn't felt in a very long time, if ever.

Amelia furrowed her brow as though she were confused, lost, and he knew he should step backward to give her some space and—politely—say to her, thank you for coming but don't tell me how to raise my own damned kid. Except he didn't want her to go. Suddenly the idea of Maria's practised flirtation sat like a noose around his neck and all he could think about was this woman's fire and spirit, her borderline hostility that was in and of itself so unusual for Santos to encounter these days—or ever.

If she'd had such an obvious reaction to the brushing of their knees, how would she feel if he kissed her? He dropped his head a little, as if weighing up the consequences of that. She smelled like honey and raspberry blossom, reminding him of the hedge along the side of this country estate, all sun-warmed and sweet.

Her eyes widened and perhaps she anticipated his intention. She lifted a hand to the front of his shirt, her fingers splayed wide over his chest, her eyes locked to his. He braced, wondering if she was about to push him away. She didn't. Her fingers buried themselves in the fabric, holding him right where he was, another breathy exhalation bursting against his jaw, then another, and another, her breathing as frantic as if she'd run a marathon. His body was hyper-charged and attuned to every single shift of hers—he felt her breath, smelled her sweet fragrance, and the tightening of her nipples into buds against his chest made him swallow a guttural groan all of his own.

This was getting out of hand.

He'd never been one for delayed gratification. What was he waiting for? A damned starter's pistol? That had been fired the second he'd opened the door and seen her standing there.

'I'm not interested in discussing my son with you, Amelia.'

Again he felt her swallowing motion. 'Why not?'

He could barely think straight. His mind was filled with the idea of kissing her, of running his tongue over the outline of her lips before plunging it deep into her warm, wet mouth. Of tangling his fingers into the back of her hair, angling her head towards his so he had unfettered access to her mouth, throat, décolletage...

Why not? It was a fair question. One he didn't want to answer.

Because all I can think of right now is you.

How ridiculous!

Her breath was warm, each little pant of air fanning against his throat. She smelled sweet.

'I care about Cameron.' Her voice was shaking as badly as her body. 'I came here because I think that he's a little boy who's had the parameters of his world shattered beyond recognition, and if you take him away from school, from his friends and me, from England, you'll make it almost impossible for him to recover.'

Her speech was fine but it barely penetrated the fog of his brain. Her eyes were pinned to his, and a silent but volatile arc of electricity buzzed from her to him.

'We cannot stay here.' He said the words for his own benefit as much as hers.

'Not for ever.' Her hand on his chest shifted, as though she didn't realise she was still touching him. She dropped it to her side but stayed where she was, their bodies hemmed together by some powerful and invisible force. 'Just until he's over this terrible grief.'

His gut rolled at that, his belly filling with pain. Terrible grief. Yes, his son was grieving and, damn it, Santos was the last person on earth who knew how to help him. Hell, Santos had no idea how to be a father, let alone the kind of father who could assist his son in navigating this kind of emotional trauma.

'I will do what I think best for my son.' It was another pledge he made more for his own benefit than for hers. In the back of his mind, he wondered why he didn't move away, why he didn't step backward, but even as he knew he ought to his body was pressing forward, his head dropping lower, as though her lips were magnetic, drawing him closer.

'Then you'll stay in England?' They were strong words but she swallowed quickly, as though her mouth was dry, her breath thick. Her lips were the palest pink, with the perfect Cupid's bow shape. He wanted to crush his own to them, to feel their softness beneath his mouth.

Her breath was forced. He had no doubt she was thinking of kissing him, just as he was her. The air seemed to spark around them, humming with an electrical current.

'And would *you* like me to stay, Miss Ashford?'

Her eyes flickered closed, long lashes fanning her cheeks for a moment, and a tiny noise escaped from her lips. Then she blinked quickly before lifting her eyes to his once more, something like panic in their depths. Her reactions were fascinating. She was like a little butterfly, flittering and moving, so fine and nimble, so difficult to pin down.

'It's not about what I want, nor what I think *you* should do.'

'Liar.' His laugh was deep and throaty, husky, as the sound brushed her hair, lifting it slightly.

It seemed to shake her, waking her from some kind of dream. Her face tightened and her features became unreadable. Her voice, when she spoke, was authoritative. Impatient, almost. 'Fine, then. *I* would like *you* to put your son before yourself. There is no doubt in my mind that leaving England suits you very nicely. It will be much easier for you to continue your life with minimal inconvenience if you return to Greece. But Cameron's interests are served by remaining right here.' And then, to underscore her feelings, she sidestepped him, moving away a little, putting vital distance between them. Something he should have done moments earlier.

Only the flush of her cheeks betrayed that she was still feeling a rush of awareness—or that she'd ever felt anything for him whatsoever. In fact, in every other way she was suddenly ice-cold.

Fascinating.

He watched her from where he was, his eyes shuttered, taking her lead and suppressing the desire that had been rampant in his system a moment ago. He wasn't sure what had come over him but it had been stupid and inappropriate. He had Maria waiting in the room next door. This woman was his son's teacher! And absolutely not his type.

Beyond that, she'd come to his home to try to organise his life—something Santos had never particularly relished.

Her small sigh drew his gaze back to her face. 'All I ask is that you think about what you would want if you were in his shoes—your whole world changing with a sadness beyond words carried inside your heart. Ask yourself what you would need and please do only that, Mr Anastakos.'

She used his surname like a shield, pressing it between them to remind him that they were two strangers, nothing more.

And she was right—he had no idea why he'd let the strength of his impulses override every piece of common sense he possessed, but he had, and it had been wrong.

'I intend on doing the right thing by him.' His admission was gravelly, his eyes reverberating with the intensity of that pledge.

'I hope so.' She stared at him for several moments and he stood perfectly still, wondering if she was going to move closer, if she was thinking about him, if she was wishing he'd given into his impulses and kissed her. But then she blinked and shook her head, forcing a tight smile to her lips.

'Enjoy your date.'

He dipped his head in what appeared to be a nod but was actually a way to disguise his thoughts.

Santos might have been called 'the billionaire playboy' for years but he lived by a strict code of conduct, a black and white morality, and that always guided how he treated women. If his father had taught him anything—and indeed he'd learned many lessons from his father's choices, most vitally how he *didn't* want to act—it was that women deserved respect. He never slept with a woman who didn't want exactly what he did and he never slept with one woman while another was waiting in a different room of the same damned house. Shame coloured his own feelings for a moment.

'Then you've said what you came to say?'

'And I hope you'll listen to it.' Her tone was ice-cold, but there was worry in it too, as though she hoped he would heed her advice but severely doubted that he would.

He held her gaze for a long time, neither of them inclined to look away, but this time he found the power to break that connection.

'Then goodnight, Miss Ashford.'

His dismissal was every bit as cold as her own words but he didn't get any satisfaction from that. Her features showed hurt and he winced inwardly, watching as she reached the door. When her hand pressed to the handle, he spoke once more, his voice gravelly. 'Thank you.' The words were stilted. She angled her face just a little, enough for him to see the proud tilt of her chin. 'For caring about Cameron, I mean.'

A cursory nod and she was gone, pulling the door behind her with a near-silent click. He stared at it for several seconds before sitting down heavily in the chair behind his desk.

Maria would keep a moment or two. Santos didn't particularly want to see her when his cock was straining against his pants, desire for another woman making him almost desperate with needs. He sat down and tried to make sense of how a slight, prim schoolteacher had driven him to the edge of sanity with little more than the sharpness of her tongue.

Amelia stared at her ceiling, completely unable to sleep. Ever since she'd walked out of Renway Hall hours earlier, she'd been unsettled and filled with a gnawing sense of frustration that made almost everything impossible.

Her body felt different. Alive on a different cos-

mic plane, existing in a hyper-aware state so everything looked and felt brighter and sharper. She'd gone
through the motions of a normal evening. A light dinner, fifteen minutes of meditation and then an hour on
the Hayashi Analysis. Usually, that consumed her, the
detailed analysis of star radius and formation stretch-
ing her brain in just the way she needed, followed by a
quick back and forth messenger chat with Brent, usually about his work or hers, before dropping into bed
exhausted and satisfied.

But not tonight.

Tonight Amelia had eaten only half her dinner, unable to fit anything else in a tummy that was already
full of knots and butterflies. Each equation she'd performed on the Hayashi Analysis had taken twice the
usual time, and she'd even found an error on one when
she'd re-read her work. She'd cut short her conversation with Brent, pleading a headache.

But she didn't have a headache. Amelia had a body
ache, deep in the pit of her abdomen, extending through
every cell of her being. She was shaking with a need
she'd never before experienced. When she closed her
eyes, she saw him. When she breathed in, she smelled
him. She lay in her bed and remembered the touch
of his finger against her lips, the feeling of his body
brushing hers. Her fingertips were still trembling as
she lifted them to her lips now, feeling the skin there.

He'd been going to kiss her; she was sure of it. She
had no experience in such matters but only a fool would
have been unable to read the signs. His head had been
lowering, his eyes rich with emotion, desire, want,

need; he'd looked at her as though he'd been dying of thirst and she the only water for miles.

Something rolled through her, the ache intensifying, her need growing, so that all she wanted was to push out of bed and return to his home, time travel be damned.

And what would he say if she turned up at his front doorstep, dressed like this?

She cast a rueful glance at her pyjamas—bearing the familiar space agency logo on the right breast, they were a size too big, and the dullest shade of grey possible. They were, she decided from her very limited contemplation on the subject, the least seductive things imaginable.

She flopped back against her pillows and continued to stare at the ceiling. She had no doubt he was supremely experienced with women. Had he sensed her inexperience? Had he realised she'd never been kissed, beyond a chaste peck on the cheek? Would he still have looked at her like that if he'd known she was a virgin?

Of course not.

The woman who'd been waiting for him had been the kind of woman he was used to—beautiful, and undoubtedly worldly and experienced. For whatever reason, perhaps he'd assumed Amelia was of that ilk.

But she wasn't. She was worlds away from that. She needed to put Santos Anastakos out of her mind, once and for all. They were oil and water—they'd never mix.

CHAPTER THREE

THE IDEA HAD come to him in the early hours of Saturday morning. After a short and frustrating evening with Maria—he was far from the perfect companion given his preoccupation with a certain schoolteacher—he'd lain awake brooding over his predicament. He deeply resented *anyone* trying to run his life—he'd been doing a damned fine job of that since he was sixteen years old—but at the same time her opinion hadn't been completely unwarranted. On the face of it, he could even admit she had a good point. But staying in England was out of the question—Santos needed to believe there was another way he could live his life and still help Cameron settle into the reality of life without his mother.

And, some time before sunrise, it had struck him: the perfect solution.

A less than ideal weekend with Cameron had cemented the plan in his mind. What had he expected—that he could turn up in Cameron's life and be instantly accepted? That they would gel immediately? Santos wasn't close to his own father—he had no real model for parental behaviour—and Cameron was a grieving, troubled boy who seemed determined to keep Santos at arm's length.

He needed help and Amelia could provide that... all he had to do was convince her of the sense of his proposal.

Santos Anastakos had been born into a fortune but before his sixteenth birthday it had almost all gone—his father's lifestyle, poor business acumen and belief that each marriage would be 'everlasting' had meant he'd failed to sign pre-nups, meaning the fortune had been divided and re-divided enough times to diminish it significantly.

Santos had restored it, piece by piece, investment by investment, so that by his twenty-fifth birthday Anastakos Inc had been the fastest growing brand in the world and his personal fortune was one of the largest. It took skill and determination, and several habits had always guided Santos. He read people and committed their traits to memory but, more importantly, he looked for their weaknesses, things he could exploit to his advantage.

Amelia had shown him her weakness and he had no doubts as to how to exploit it to get exactly what he wanted. The ends justified the means, though—they had to. He was sinking, with no idea what to say or how to behave with his own damned son. For a man who commanded any room he entered, the complete lack of power made him feel impotent. He hated it.

He'd never wanted children; he'd been very careful to avoid having children—or so he'd believed. Nonetheless, Cameron was in existence, a six-year-old boy who was the spitting image of Santos at around the same age. His eyes were unmistakable—it was like looking in a miniature mirror. The DNA test he'd flown to England prepared to organise had been rendered unnecessary from the first meeting. Cameron was his son.

All that was left to do was work out *how* to be a father. People talked about parenting instincts but Santos had none. He didn't really like children—they were illogical and emotional, demanding. And yet there *was* something else, something he hadn't expected: a kind of soul-deep connection. He looked at Cameron and felt a link to his past, as though a part of himself had been severed from his body and become independent. He also felt an overwhelming fear: fear of ruining Cameron's life; of hurting him; of making him miserable; and, yes, of compounding the grief he was feeling now; fear that he wouldn't be the father Cameron needed—that he wasn't capable of being any kind of father.

He was terrified that his son would come to hate him.

He ruminated on this as he waited in his car, watching the entrance to the school. It was a nice enough school, he conceded, though far from what he might have chosen had he known he was a father. Cynthia had enrolled him in the local comprehensive—because anything else had been beyond her budget. The area was good, though, the buildings quaint in that English style and the street he was parked in lined with leafy trees.

Something shifted in the periphery of his vision and he responded immediately, training his gaze on the movement: Amelia. He pressed his hand to the door handle, preparing to step out.

But, for just a moment, he watched her. It was another warm day and today she was wearing a dress. Pale grey with an intricate pattern—perhaps flowers— it wrapped around her chest and tied at the waist, drawing attention to her gentle curves, the roundness of her breasts and neatness of her waist, so the same torpedo of attraction was spiralling through him, unwelcome and completely unwanted.

He wasn't here to notice her damned figure, no matter how tempting he found it. More important considerations were at stake. Cameron had barely spoken to Santos since coming to stay with him, but when he had it had all been about Miss Ashford.

'Miss Ashford this...'

'Miss Ashford that...'

'Miss Ashford makes me feel happy...'

'Miss Ashford understands me...'

'Miss Ashford says...'

And on and on and on.

It had been a little irritating before but, now that he'd met Miss Ashford for himself, it was downright distracting. He didn't need any help putting that woman front and centre of his mind. All weekend he'd found his thoughts straying to her, remembering the husky little breath she'd made up close, the way her lips had parted when he'd moved close, as though silently inviting him to kiss her. To the way her eyes had rolled back at the simple touch of his fingertip to her lips, almost as though she'd been on the brink of an orgasm from the light, meaningless flirtation.

And he'd wondered about what would have happened if he'd acted more swiftly, kissing her as soon as he'd wanted to rather than trying to fight his desire. She'd been doing the same exercise, he was certain of it, and she'd triumphed in a way he hadn't. She'd put an end to the preamble—for surely it had been? Another minute and his mouth would have claimed hers, his lips dominating hers…and then?

Yes, that was where he came unstuck, because 'and then' was a slippery slope to the kind of fantasies that made it hard for him to watch Miss Ashford even at this distance without feeling a stirring in his groin.

Pushing out of the car with a determined tilt of his head, Santos strode across the street, arriving at her side before she'd even registered his presence. She glanced up at him and, at the moment of realisation, made a husky noise of acknowledgement that almost skittled the carefully thought out proposal he was about to make, given how much it reminded him of Friday night.

'Miss Ashford.' He couldn't help it. The words were drawled with a hint of sensuality, so her pupils darkened and her cheeks filled with that ready blush once more.

'Mr Anastakos.' She took a step back, her eyes failing to meet his. Didn't she realise how crazy that made him?

'I need to speak with you.'

'Oh?' Her brows drew together and her hands fidgeted with her car keys. 'You do? About what?'

It was an artless response and inwardly he smiled. If she thought he'd come to talk about their obvious chemistry then it proved she was at least as aware of it as he. It was a short-lived triumph. Desire for this woman would only complicate what he needed, and he was quite certain now that she was essential to his plan.

'Cameron.' Her expression shifted speculatively at the mention of the young boy. She hadn't been expecting that. 'Do you have a moment?'

'I…' Her teeth dragged on her lower lip and her body swayed a little, tiny gestures of temptation that didn't escape his notice. 'If it's a parent-teacher interview then I suggest you make an appointment through the headmaster's office.'

His smile was laced with scepticism. She'd already shown him how deeply she cared for Cameron. Her objection was weak at best, born of a desire not to act on the crazy, sensual impulses that were fogging them both. 'It's important.'

He could feel her prevaricating and then, finally, she sighed. 'Fine. What is it?'

He gestured towards a bench, a little way down the path in the shade of a considerable elm tree.

'That's okay. I don't have long right now so I suggest you cut right to it.' She cast a glance at her wristwatch, a small frown pulling at her features. The statement pushed under his skin, making him wonder where she was going, making him wonder a great many things: what was her life like, what did she do outside of school?

'I've thought about your objections to my plans.'

Her eyes clearly showed surprise.

'You weren't expecting that?'

'Frankly? No.'

'Why not?'

'Honestly?'

'Always.' It was a husky encouragement.

She bit down on her lower lip as she thought about that. 'You don't strike me as the kind of man who would change his mind.'

'No?'

She shook her head. 'You seem too arrogant for that.'

His brows shifted upwards and she clamped a hand over her mouth, her eyes sweetly apologetic. Sweetly? What the hell...?

'Oh, I still believe taking Cameron to Agrios Nisi is the correct decision.' He spoke firmly, allaying any relief she might have felt.

Her features shifted, sparking with the defiance that was instantly familiar.

'Then you haven't changed your mind?'

'No.'

'Oh.' Her disappointment was obvious, her full lips instinctively dropping into a small frown, and he repressed an impulse to wipe his thumb across her lower lip once more to remind himself of how soft and sweet they felt beneath his touch. As if she could read his mind, she lifted her own fingers to her lower lip, tracing the outline there. It was almost painful to watch her reciprocate, so he jabbed his hands in his pockets, focussing on his reasons for being here.

'I do not want to make Cameron's life harder than it needs to be. I am, naturally, mindful of what he's been through, and for how that's affecting him. I concede that these changes must be overwhelming to the boy and, like you, I want to protect him.'

'You do?' Her brow furrowed, her lip dropping further. His body tightened in an immediate and unwelcome response.

'Of course. Do you think I'm some kind of monster? That I'd revel in my own son's pain?'

'I didn't mean that.' Her cheeks bloomed into a pink the colour of plum blossoms.

'Didn't you?'

He scanned her face—not dowdy, not even remotely. 'Considered' would be a better word. Measured. Everything about her was carefully audited, even her reaction in his office. Desire had been swamping them both but she'd pulled herself back, wrapping herself in a veneer of ice, pushing him away before things could get out of hand. Her control was impressive. Or perhaps he was just surprised to meet a woman who wasn't vying to be taken to bed by him. It had been many years since he'd been turned down—if ever. It was little wonder the experience had dominated his thoughts since. It was the novelty factor.

'No!' Her denial was emphatic. 'But moving him to Greece is, in my opinion, going to be very difficult for him.'

'And you don't want that.'

'No.' Her voice softened, the hint of a smile curving her lips. 'I—I told you the other night...' She stumbled awkwardly over the words. 'I care for Cameron very deeply. I understand the position is awkward for both of you but *you're* the adult. It's your job to protect him.'

'And I intend to.' His eyes sparked with hers, narrowing speculatively. 'Which brings me to why I'm here.'

She waited, silent, her eyes boring into his now, her

lips parted ever so slightly. He wished she wouldn't do that.

'I have a proposition for you.'

Her eyes grew more round, her lips parting further as she whooshed out a deep breath. 'Go on,' she prompted, though it sounded as if she'd rather do just about anything than hear whatever was coming next.

'Come with us.'

She blinked, shaking her head a little. 'What do you mean?'

'At the end of the school year, I will take Cameron to my island to live. Come with him and help him to adjust to his new life. Help him adjust to me.' The final request surprised him; he hadn't planned to admit how hard he was finding it to bond with his son, nor to forgive Cynthia for keeping their child a secret. Whenever he looked at Cameron he could see only what he'd missed out on, not what he'd gained.

'You're asking me to go to Agrios Nisi with you?'

'I'm offering you a job,' he clarified. 'Six weeks as Cameron's companion.'

Amelia frowned, again shaking her head a little. 'He has a nanny.'

'He's had three nannies since his mother died but, yes, right now he has a nanny and she seems competent. I think he probably likes her better than the other two. However, she is a career nanny. While she takes excellent care of him, I don't feel that she has much of a personal connection with Cameron. You apparently do.'

Amelia looked sideways a moment, lifting a hand and brushing her hair from her face. She wore on her middle finger a gold ring with a flat face, the kind of ring one might get at a college graduation ceremony. He didn't recognise the engraving; and she moved her hand again, much too quickly for him to commit the design to memory.

'I think Cameron is a very unique little boy and what he's been through…' Her voice tapered off a little, her eyes suspiciously moist. But when she turned back to face him there was a strength in her eyes, a look of determination. 'I care for all my students, Mr Anastakos.'

'But particularly for Cameron.'

She bit down on her lower lip, anguish in her eyes. He could feel her prevarication, her torment. She wanted to accept his offer but she was scared. Of what—him? Of what happened between them the other night?

'This would be a formal offer of employment,' he said smoothly. 'My lawyer would arrange a contract, you'd be paid a salary—given set hours and weekends—just like a regular job.' And then, after a pause, 'I would expect nothing of you personally.'

He saw his words affecting her, drawing her out, and she made a noise of consideration.

'I don't know. On the one hand, I'd do anything for Cameron, but…'

'But?' He challenged, though he knew the answer. Their chemistry frightened her. For whatever reason, the strength of desire that had arced between them wasn't something she wanted to indulge—ever.

Desperation drove him to tighten the screws regardless. 'Let's be clear: my plans will not change. One way or another, in two weeks I will take Cameron with me, away from here. If you care about him, and want to help ease him through the transition period, then accept my offer.'

She sucked in a sharp breath. 'You know, this runs pretty darned close to emotional blackmail.'

His expression didn't shift but he was left wondering in what way this didn't constitute full-blown emotional blackmail.

She flicked a glance at her wristwatch. 'I have to go.'

Something uncomfortably like panic had him reaching for her wrist, his fingers curving around her fine bones, his thumb padding over her skin before he could stop himself. 'Wait.' The word emerged as a deep, husky command. 'You haven't given me an answer.'

'Do I get to think about it?'

'Do you need to think about it?'

She pulled her hand away, rubbing her wrist; her eyes holding his were awash with doubts. 'I would have conditions.'

'Go on.' He dropped her hand, stepping backward, crossing his arms over his chest. He forced himself to give her the entirety of his concentration.

'I have work commitments outside of the school. I'd need an office for my use.'

That sparked his curiosity—hell, it ignited it into a full-blown fireball—but he knew better than to probe her further at this point. Once she was on the island, he could ask her all sorts of questions, if he found she still held his interest. Not now, while her acceptance was in the balance.

'That is not a problem.'

'Okay.' She chewed on her lip in a way that drove him utterly crazy.

'Okay? You'll do it?'

She stopped nodding and frowned. 'Okay, I'll think about it. Send me a contract and I'll advise your lawyers as to my response.'

CHAPTER FOUR

She had to be crazy. For two weeks she'd back-flipped on this, wondering at her acceptance of this summer job—which was how she'd taken to thinking of it, the only way she could deal with what she'd accepted without going into a full-blown panic.

It was just work. A temporary assignment. And, more than that, it was an opportunity to help Cameron get through another trauma in his life. She knew what change was like for children—how many times had she been forced to move, to meet new people, to accept new teachers, homes, experiences? Her childhood had been marked by extreme loneliness, a state of utter sadness and displacement almost all the time, all set against a backdrop that making her parents proud was the only way she could make them love her.

People didn't seem to realise that having a very high IQ didn't obviate the normal developmental milestones. Amelia had been plagued by nightmares as a child, one in particular—being consumed by a void, an impenetrable darkness that filled her lungs with bleakness and a weight of despair from which she could never escape. Whenever she'd experienced that terror she'd woken and cried for her mother—but she'd never been there. Often, there had been no one who could comfort her.

Loneliness was familiar to Amelia and she hated that Cameron was going through that now. She wanted to comfort him and *that* was why she'd agreed to this. It wasn't the exorbitant amount Santos was paying her—her consulting work paid well; she didn't need the money. And it certainly wasn't for any other personal consideration. Santos was no draw-card whatsoever. If anything, he was a disincentive, a reason to refuse his offer.

But Cameron overrode every single one of those concerns. So here she was, holding the little boy's hand as the helicopter circled lower over an island that was beyond anything she could have imagined. Lush greenery grew quite wild over most of it, with a small village in the north and pristine, white sand all around. The water that lapped at the island's edges was aquamarine.

As the helicopter came down lower, Amelia picked out an enormous house right on the water's edge, rendered in white with miles of tinted glass, making it impossible to see into it. The house was a testament to modern architecture, all clean lines and simple aesthetic. There was a swimming pool, several tennis courts, a fruit grove, a golf course and, as she looked towards the water, she saw a jetty at which were moored a yacht and several smaller crafts—speedboats and jet skis lined up side by side.

A curl of derision escaped onto her lips before she could contain it—of course a playboy like Santos had all the toys to go with the title.

She told herself that the butterflies in her tummy

had to do with the rapid descent towards the island and nothing whatsoever to do with the fact that soon she would see him again. Santos. She knew from Cameron that Santos had travelled to the island a few days ago, leaving the little boy in the care of his nanny, Talia. Amelia had suppressed her disapproval. Now that she was here, she could see some stability for Cameron's life.

The helicopter came in even lower, and beside her Cameron was very still and watchful. She angled her face, something clutching in the region of her heart. The first time she'd seen the little boy, he'd looked a bit like this. Far less well-dressed; his uniform had been stained—second-hand, Amelia had gathered— and quite ill-fitting. His face, though, had held a familiar sense of awe, and she'd understood it. He'd been starting nursery and she'd been doing her first teacher's assistant rotation—she'd told him she was nervous too, and that perhaps they'd feel better if they sat side by side.

He'd moved into different classes over the last few years but she'd always kept an eye out for him and had welcomed him to her class this year with absolute delight. Seeing his grief at the shocking death of his mother had hit Amelia right in the chest—she'd cried with him, for him, and on that first night had wished she could bundle him into her arms and take him home. The instinct had surprised her.

Amelia wasn't maternal. Her childhood had been as far removed from 'normal' as was possible. She had no idea how to be someone's parent, and no desire to be either. But there was something about Cameron with his soulful blue-grey eyes that had buried itself deep into her heart. Not loving him wasn't an option. It wasn't permitted to have favourite students, and she'd taken great care not to show a preference, but that hadn't meant she didn't feel it.

The same nervousness and anxiety she'd sensed in him as a slender little three-year-old was in his face now. She put a hand on his knee reassuringly and squeezed. 'The island looks beautiful.'

He turned to face her, those eyes that she'd fallen in love with haunting her now, because it was impossible not to see his father in their depths. They were identical—the same shape and colour, each set rimmed with thick, curling lashes. But this wasn't about Santos Anastakos. That wasn't why she'd accepted this job. It was all for Cameron.

'It looks hot.'

'You don't like the heat?'

He lifted his shoulders and turned away from her, his fragility palpable despite his above-average height. 'No. Not really.'

Amelia smiled but it was forced onto her face. She didn't particularly like the heat either but they'd both have to tolerate it for this summer. The helicopter touched down on the roof of the house and a moment later a man appeared, followed by a woman. Both were dressed in immaculate steel-grey suits.

'Miss Ashford,' the man greeted her, shouting to be heard over the whir of the spinning helicopter blades. She dipped her head forward as the helicopter pilot had instructed her to do, clutching Cameron's hand in her own, guiding him down the steps and away from the aircraft. The heat hit her like a wave in the face, sultry and thick, the air so warm it burst flame into her lungs.

'Yes?' she said when they were at a safe distance. Talia, the nanny, followed behind.

'I'm Leo.' He smiled, a kindly smile that matched his bearing. He wasn't much taller than her, though there was a tautness to him, a strength she could feel emanating from his muscular frame. 'I run security on the island and for Mr Anastakos generally. I'll be coordinating things for Cameron.'

'Things?' Amelia prompted impatiently.

'Security for any day trips, routines, that sort of thing.' He spoke with a Greek accent, though it was different from Santos's.

Amelia compressed her lips, ignoring the shift of disapproval. Given what Santos was worth, it wasn't entirely unreasonable that there should be some kind of security measure for Cameron yet it was just another adjustment for the young boy to make.

'I presume that here on the island he won't need too much?'

'No,' he agreed. 'This place is a fortress.'

She arched a brow. 'A fortress you can reach by air or sea?' She gestured to the expansive ocean surrounding the island.

'Under surveillance,' he amended with a grin.

'I'm Chloe.' The woman behind him reached around to shake Amelia's hand. 'I run the house.'

Amelia nodded, wondering at the grandness of that—having a housekeeper and a security manager. It didn't surprise her, and yet she couldn't imagine living in such a fashion.

That feeling only increased as she was shown through the house. It was undeniably beautiful, and built right on the edge of the beach, so an infinity pool and terrace gave way to white sand and then pristine ocean. All of the rooms were on a large scale, with high ceilings, more impressive artwork adorning the crisp, white walls.

Cameron's room—or suite of rooms—made her heart clutch. No expense had been spared, but it was more than that. Whoever had overseen the decorating had done so with care. The books were perfectly chosen for a child his age, the toys likewise. There wasn't a cacophony of plastic. Instead, it was wooden blocks and construction toys, a selection of board games and paints. She inwardly approved of the selection, though she couldn't help but feel the stark contrast with the way Cameron had been living previously. She knew from brief conversations with Cynthia that their home had been a small flat above the high street where the smell of the fish and chip shop below had infiltrated each of the rooms with its greasy pungency. There was only one bedroom—Cameron's. Cynthia had slept on a fold-out sofa in the lounge.

It was hard not to judge Santos for that—for leaving the mother of his child to suffer in such abject poverty. Was it really possible he hadn't known about Cameron?

Compressing her lips on that thought, and attempting to blot Santos from her mind, she completed the tour with Talia and Cameron. When Talia suggested taking Cameron to the kitchen for a snack, Amelia was secretly pleased. She felt overwhelmed with what she'd done; the enormity of stranding herself on this island with a man like Santos Anastakos had her wanting to beg the helicopter pilot to fly her right back to the mainland airport.

But she didn't.

Cameron's face swam before her eyes and all her doubts left her. She was right to be here. He needed this of her.

As it turned out, her anxiety was somewhat misplaced. After Cameron had a snack, she watched Talia and him swim, then joined them in a game of Snakes and Ladders before finishing a few chapters of a book in her room. She read Cameron his bedtime story and sat with him as he fell asleep—he hadn't asked her to but she'd sensed his sadness, understood that essential loneliness and wanted to comfort him as best she could.

She ate alone—the housekeeper Chloe had prepared some chicken and salad. Afterwards, Amelia took a cup of tea onto the terrace along with her book and curled her knees beneath her chin as she watched the sun set, the sky filling with a sensational mix of colours—purple, gold, orange, the beginning of berry-black. Despite all that she knew about the formation of the universe, and the metaphysics behind the sunset, she could never fail to be awed by the repetitive cosmic phenomenon, and particularly not when it took place over a seemingly limitless ocean.

It was dark by the time she'd finished her tea. She stood and moved into the kitchen, washed the cup and placed it on the side of the sink before filling a water glass to take to her bedroom. Carrying it and her book—a heavy hardback—she walked from the kitchen, her eyes flicking towards the night sky beyond on autopilot. The stars shone so brightly here, it made Amelia long for her telescope.

She wasn't looking where she was going, and apparently neither was he, because a second later Amelia connected not with a wall or a door but with a solid shape that knocked her backward. Her water spilled all over Santos's chest, covering his shirt in a spreading pool of liquid.

'Oh!' Her eyes dropped to his chest and couldn't look away. The water made every sculpted delineation visible. His torso was ridged with abdominal muscles, just like the statues of Greek gods she'd studied as a girl.

'I'm so sorry!' The words stumbled from her mouth and she briefly risked a glance at his face, then wished she hadn't. Fire seemed to arc from his eyes to hers, his perfectly shaped lips flattening into a line that could have represented disapproval, impatience or irritation. Far better to believe that than anything else.

She swallowed hard, trying to bring moisture back to her dry mouth.

'Let me...' She pressed her hand against his shirt, intending only to wipe away the water, but the same flames spiralled through her at the slight contact. 'Get you a towel,' she finished, spinning away from him quickly so she could retrieve something from the kitchen. Only she bumped into the edge of the kitchen door in her haste and embarrassment, and squawked awkwardly at the pain that flooded her.

Amelia closed her eyes on a wave of mortification. *Great. Just great.*

'Is there anything else you'd like to walk into?' he asked and, heaven help her, Amelia had somehow managed to forget the deep huskiness of his voice, the sultry heat of his accent. It wrapped around her now, making thought and words impossible.

Amelia had begun speaking in full sentences at six months of age—apparently one of the first markers for an unusually high IQ—but in that moment she struggled to wrap her brain around a single word whatsoever.

She made do with firing him a terse smile then continued her trajectory—more carefully this time—into the kitchen, rifling through drawers until she found a tea towel. Spinning round to take it to Santos, she realised he'd followed her into the kitchen and was in the process of unbuttoning his shirt.

Good Lord. Her mouth was drier than the desert.

'Oh.' She stared at him. 'You're getting undressed.'

His grin was rich with amusement. 'I'm removing a wet shirt. It's not quite the same thing.'

'Isn't it?' It sure *felt* the same. 'I was just…going to bed.' Oh, no! That sounded like an invitation! She furrowed her brow, shaking her head a little. What the heck was happening to her? 'To read.'

'Do you have everything you need?'

She lifted her book. 'Yes.'

His smile was slow to spread but her reaction was instant. Her skin prickled all over with tiny darts of heat. 'I meant in the house. Did Chloe show you where everything is?'

Amelia nodded. 'Yes. She did.' And then, with a small shake of her head, 'Though not an office I can use.'

'Would you like to see it now?'

Her chest tightened. She did—she wanted to start her work routine the next day, and knowing exactly where she could work from would be vital to that, but the naked chest of Santos Anastakos was almost too much to bear. 'Would you like to get…erm…dressed first?'

'Would *you* like me to get dressed first?' He put the question back on her and somehow managed to make her feel like a child. Naïve and gauche. She shook her head and tried to look cool, as though she frequently spent time with half-naked, bronzed living replicas of sculpted Greek gods.

'That's fine.' She shrugged with an assumed and not entirely credible air of nonchalance. 'Which way?'

'Did you want to refill your water glass first?'

Heat stained her cheeks. She shook her head—she could come back later. He took a step backward, allowing her space to precede him from the kitchen, and she skirted past him, ever so careful not to so much as brush his skin. If he noticed, he didn't say anything, though she was sure she caught the tail end of a smile on his face when she glanced up at him.

'How was your flight?'

'Fine.' She lifted her shoulders. 'It was my first time in a private jet.'

'I thought it would be easier with Cameron.'

'He travelled well.' She fell into step beside him, feeling a little calmer as they moved onto safer conversational ground. 'He was excited by the helicopter.'

Santos's expression was distracted. 'I thought he might be.'

'Where do you work?'

'I have an office here.'

'On the island?'

'Yes.' He dipped his head forward. 'Though I travel to Athens most days. We have headquarters there and I usually have meetings that require my personal attention.'

Amelia's brow furrowed as she digested this. 'So you won't be here much?'

He fixed her with an enquiring gaze.

'I mean long-term. With Cameron.'

Santos's pace slowed to a stop. 'You're asking if I intend to neglect my son?'

Heat flowed in her cheeks. 'I—'

'You have a habit of seeing the worst in me, when it comes to him.'

'Do I?'

'You think I've moved him here and plan never to see him?'

'If today is any indication.'

'I work long hours.' He expelled a breath so his nostrils flared. 'Up until three months ago I had no idea I was a father. I am *intending* to make whatever changes are necessary to fit Cameron into my life but it will take time. Forgive me, Miss Ashford, for not having all the answers just yet.'

She felt a small shift of sympathy for him, but an even greater one for Cameron; after her own childhood she knew the facts Santos was failing to see. 'So long as you love him, above anything and anyone else, you'll work it out.'

The words seemed to lash Santos. He shifted a little, a physical reaction—a rejection?—and then began to walk once more, his stride longer this time, his face glowering.

'This area is generally off-limits to my domestic staff.' He didn't look at her. 'It will also be off-limits to Cameron and Talia. I work on sensitive projects. I require privacy and peace.'

Amelia's stomach squeezed. He was changing the subject, but she didn't want him to do that. She reached for his arm, ignoring the tingling wave that crashed through her at the small touch. 'Santos?'

He stopped walking, turning to face her without meeting her eyes, his nostrils flaring as he expelled a deep breath.

'You don't agree with me?'

Now his eyes dragged to hers, slowly, something dark in their depths. 'About…?'

But he understood. He was evading her question on purpose. 'You don't need to overthink things with Cameron. In time, and with an abundance of love, he'll find his way to you.'

A muscle jerked low in his jaw. 'And if I cannot give him those things?'

'What do you mean?' She lifted a brow, impatient for him to explain.

'You think it's so easy? You simply say "love the child" and it is done? A matter of months ago, I didn't even know about him.'

Defence of Cameron raised her hackles. 'So? That's not his fault. You're his father.'

'Whatever that means.' He spun round, walking once more, his stride long, not stopping until he reached an office door beside the one he'd indicated as his.

'From time to time my assistant flies to the island to work with me—she uses this space. In her absence, consider it yours.' It was a swift conversation change but she allowed it, seeing the futility in pushing him further at this point.

Amelia looked around the room—yet again, on a rather grand scale—and nodded. Two computer screens sat side by side on a large desk. Another desk, free of any clutter or technology, was set at a right angle to it, forming an L shape in which a comfortable looking black leather chair was anchored. A leather armchair sat across the room and the walls were lined with bookshelves.

'I presume this will suffice?'

'Yes,' she agreed, noting the things it had and those it did not, while her mind analysed his throwaway comment 'whatever that means'.

'But it's lacking something?'

Was she so transparent? 'No, it will be fine.'

'You're easier to read than a book. What do you need?'

She bit down on her lower lip but promptly stopped when his gaze was drawn to the gesture, overheating her already frantic blood. 'A whiteboard.'

He nodded crisply. 'Of course. I suppose as a teacher you're used to writing vertically.'

It took her a moment to connect her vocation with this work. 'Right.' She cleared her throat.

'I'll have Leo arrange one for you in the morning.'

'I don't want to put him to any trouble.'

'It's not a problem.'

'Well, not for you,' she pointed out, surprising them

both with the joke. His smile was instinctive, but it died almost instantly. He stared at her for several moments and she felt as though he was choosing his words carefully.

'What if I can't love him?'

Amelia's eyebrows shot up. 'You're serious?'

His features were like stone as he nodded once. *'Nai.'*

'Oh, Santos.' She was so swept up in his worry that it didn't occur to her to use his surname. 'You *will.* Not just because he's your son, but because he's an amazing little boy. Open yourself up to the possibility of loving him and it will happen without you realising it.'

'Your confidence is naïve.'

She blinked, trying to remember the last time anyone had said anything even remotely approaching an aspersion cast on her intelligence.

'I can only assume your own childhood was a picture of rosy parental doting, but that's not the norm for many people. I am not close to my father. Nor is my brother. In my family, "love" is very far from how we do it. So how can you expect me to open myself to the possibility of loving him? How can I ever replace the mother he lost? I'm simply not built that way. *Christos*, I chose to not have children for this very reason, Amelia.'

She flinched a little, wanting to refute his assumption about her and his words about himself. Her childhood had been far from what he believed. But his own summation of his life and choices filled her with such sadness. His uncertainty was so unexpected that she was lost for words.

He spoke before she could, anyway.

'Regardless, he is my son, and I will care for him to the best of my ability. I will raise him so that he wants for nothing it is within my power to provide. But do not expect miracles while you are here. Your concern is my son's happiness, not his relationship with me.'

CHAPTER FIVE

AMELIA SLEPT FITFULLY and woke early. Santos had filled her dreams. He'd overtaken every single one of them, his words filling her with a strange heaviness.

She wasn't sure why his confession had caught her off-guard. Because he seemed so confident, so ruthlessly capable of anything he set his mind to? Or because he'd echoed one of her own deeply held fears? Her parents had hardly given her a shining example of what family life should be like, yet deep down, despite that, she knew that the love between a child and parent was generally inviolable.

Santos would see that. He *had* to.

Throwing back the lightweight cover, she pushed out of bed and padded across the room to the enormous windows that overlooked the ocean. Waves tumbled towards the shore in the cool dawn light. There was no heat accompanying the sun—yet—though she knew it would come.

But for the moment, the view beyond the window was so tantalising she didn't think twice. Pausing only to pull on a simple cotton dress and some sandals, she slipped out of her room, quietly moving through the enormous house that, at this early hour, seemed to be almost completely asleep. Which suited her perfectly.

She opened the glass doors just enough to slide between them, then almost ran towards the water. How long had it been since she'd swum in the sea? Years. Not since she was last in Cape Canaveral.

A smile lifted her lips as the tiled deck gave way to the cool sand, crunchy underfoot, and she could smell the tang of salt in the air. At the water's edge she slowed but kept moving forward. The water was warmer than she'd expected and she walked up to her knees; then, chancing a look over her shoulder towards the house to reassure herself that she was completely alone, she tucked her dress into the elastic hips of her underpants and went deeper still. It was the most sublime feeling—she wished she'd taken a little longer to change into bathers. Tomorrow, she'd know better. The idea of floating on her back as the waves rolled beneath her was almost too tempting.

With a small sigh, she began to walk parallel to the coastline, staying mid-thigh-depth, so each step required her to push through the water. The exercise felt good, the weight of the water a pleasant obstacle.

The coastline on the island was flat here, but only ten minutes or so later the sand gave way to small dunes that morphed into hills and finally cliff-faces, white with tufts of green sprouting through them. She eyed them with curiosity, wondering at the stones in their formation. Cliffs on islands like this tended to boast caves and naturally occurring dens. She wondered if there were any here. If she followed the water round, would she find a disused pirate sanctuary? The idea had her curiosity piqued and she walked on, further than she'd intended, until the wall of the cliff jutted out far enough to make further exploration impossible. She looked upward, the sheer size of the rock wall causing her to hold her breath a moment.

It would be impossible to explore without a swimming costume—and possibly without a boat. Putting it on the 'another time' list, she turned and began the walk back to the house, this time wading through water that was a little shallower, up to her calves.

The sun was just fully bursting into the sky by the time she reached a place in the water that was parallel with house. She stood for a moment with her back to the ocean, simply staring at the beautiful property. Had he built it? Or had his father? It was modern in style but it could still have been built anywhere from the fifties and refurbished over the years. While it was beautiful, it was isolated, and she wondered about that too. Did he feel lonely here? Or did he like that?

And why did she care? With a small groan, she began to move back towards the house, deciding coffee was in order. She scooped down to pick up her sandals from where she'd slipped out of them and carried them the rest of the way. On the terrace, she moved her feet back and forth, trying to get the sand off, before looking around for a tap.

'It's over there.' His voice ran down her spine, seductive and warm, but despite that she shivered, an involuntary tremble that made her legs a little unsteady. She looked at Santos as he gestured towards a tap, only his eyes remained on her, tracing the outline of her legs that must have been visible beneath the flimsy fabric of her dress.

'Thank you.' Her heart was rabbiting hard against her ribcage but she kept walking until she reached the tap, then switched it on, slowly cleaning her feet of all sand and sucking in air before she lifted to standing and spun to face him once more. He'd been angry the night before, rude and hostile.

Remember that, she cautioned herself, even as her body was already responding to his.

'I didn't know anyone else was up,' she explained a little caustically. 'I didn't mean to disturb you.'

He turned to face her, pinning her with the full force of his crystal-clear ice blue eyes. 'Didn't you?'

She pressed her teeth into her lower lip. 'Of course not.'

His response was a small shift of his mouth—she might have called it a sneer, except it lacked acerbity— and then lifted a coffee cup. 'Join me. The pot is still warm.' In truth, she was desperate for a coffee, but with Santos?

Perhaps her uncertainty expressed itself because he made a small sound of impatience. 'It's just coffee.'

Her eyes flared wide, clashing with his, and her stomach rolled in response. 'Fine. Thank you.' Her smile was strained. 'I can't function without the stuff.'

He nodded in agreement, moved inside for a moment to retrieve another cup then returned, filling it and handing it to her. She was careful not to allow even a hint of contact between their fingers when she took it from him, and at close proximity didn't quite meet his eyes.

She took a drink and then pulled a face, looking at him to see mirth in his eyes.

'It's very strong,' she said unnecessarily.

'It's Greek.'

'And all Greek things are strong?' She'd intended it to come out as a joke, but the close proximity to Santos had robbed her of the ability to sound anything but breathy. What was happening to her? Amelia had lectured at Ivy League schools when she'd been fifteen years old. Why did the presence of this man turn her into someone who could barely speak?

'And irresistible.' His words were teasing but there was an undercurrent to them that pulled at her belly, making it impossible to smile in response. She took another sip of the coffee, grateful for having something to do with her hands, anything that might make it look as though she wasn't affected by being this close to him; as though she didn't wish she'd stayed in his office that night rather than high-tailing it out of there as quickly as she could.

For goodness' sake! They hadn't even kissed that night! He'd moved close to her and he'd looked at her as though he'd *wanted* to. But for Santos Anastakos, famed playboy bachelor, that was probably just how he was wired. The kind of encounter that happened to him often. It was highly likely he'd put her from his mind as soon as she'd left his office—why in the world would she expect otherwise? Just because he'd become a constant figment of her thoughts and fantasies ever since was no indication of how he'd been affected by... by what? Standing close to one another in his office?

She felt completely juvenile to have invested such a simple thing with so much importance.

He'd had a beautiful woman waiting for him—Amelia had had to scurry past her to vacate his home. Had she spent the night with him? The thought eroded the lining of Amelia's stomach, filling it with a hint of acid, and now her eyes did lift to his, staying there for several seconds. Of course she had! This was Santos Anastakos. The man was rumoured to live and breathe affairs.

'Who was that woman?'

Had he moved closer? She felt as though he was pressing to her, but he wasn't. It was just an atmospheric compression—not physically possible, given their matter states, but she could have sworn it was happening. 'Which woman?'

'Maria,' she supplied, conjuring a mental image of the stunning creature, all long legs and glossy hair.

A small frown pulled at his lips. 'A friend.'

Something a lot like relief burst through Amelia. It spelled trouble and disaster and a thousand other portents of ill that she knew she should pay attention to. Standing here with him like this was madness—nothing good could come from indulging a desire to be close to him. She was fighting with fire, but found she couldn't step away.

'Just a friend?' she asked, wondering what he must think of her, seeking reassurance over something like this.

Another small frown brushed over his features. 'Yes.'

She bit down on her lip, wishing that revelation didn't affect her.

'We were seeing each other for a time. We catch up occasionally, when it suits us both.'

Amelia had barely any experience with men, and precisely zero with men like Santos, but she gathered 'seeing each other' and 'catch up' were euphemistic terms hinting at a physical relationship.

Amelia's face was unknowingly expressive, her features contorting to show her discomfort. Only someone completely lacking in intuitive skills would have failed to understand the direction of her thoughts.

'I had my driver take her back to London after dinner,' he said quietly, and now she knew she wasn't imagining it. He moved closer, his legs brushing hers, the small cup filled with thick Greek coffee the only barrier between them. 'And dinner was somewhat rushed.' A smile that was hard to analyse. Self-deprecating? Annoyed?

She shook her head, needing to put an end to this. It had taken all her strength in his office; if she wasn't careful, she'd lose herself completely to this sense of madness. 'It's none of my business. I shouldn't have asked.'

'But you did.'

She nodded, searching for an excuse.

'Because that night in my office, if you hadn't moved away from me, I would have kissed you.'

She was drowning all over again, trying to draw in air and failing. She had no idea how to respond to that.

'And I don't think we would have stopped at a kiss, Miss Ashford.' Her name was a slow, sensual seduction on his lips. It shimmied through her, threatening to mould her into something new and unrecognisable.

Her skin was covered in goose bumps, her blood rushing in anticipation and hope—she needed him to touch her. She needed him to kiss her, just as he'd said he'd wanted to. God help her, she was losing herself to him, to the ocean, the endless sea, of possibilities.

She angled her face to his, her lips parted in an unspoken invitation, her eyes wide. 'What would have happened, Santos?' She liked using his name. It was a leveller of sorts, making her feel like his equal instead of a woefully inexperienced child.

Something flared in his gaze, a heat that pooled lava in the pit of her abdomen. His hands curled around her coffee cup, lifting it to her lips so she could take a sip, then placing it on the table behind them without moving away from her at all. 'I would have made love to you.'

So simple, so erotic.

Her eyes swept shut on the imagery it conveyed, on the very idea of that! Where she should have been glad she'd broken the strange tension that had imprisoned them both, she felt only remorse now. What would it have been like to experience that?

'I would have stripped your clothes from your body until you were naked and trembling.' His fingers brushed her thighs, just beneath the hem of her dress. 'And I would have kissed you everywhere, tasting you, driving you to the brink of insanity before making you mine in every way.' He dropped his head and his lips brushed hers so briefly she thought she'd imagined it; but, no, there was an explosive feeling against her flesh that showed it had been real. A pulse ran the length of her spine.

He moved his mouth towards her ear, speaking low

and soft. 'The first time would have been fast. I needed you too much to take it slowly. But afterwards, I would have carried you upstairs to my room, laid you naked in my bed and spent the night devouring you, not letting you sleep, not letting you breathe except to scream my name.'

'Santos.' The word was a hopeless surrender, thready and soft. She wasn't sure if she was imploring him to stop speaking that way or to speak less and *do* more but she whispered his name beseechingly.

She needed to regain her sanity, to keep hold of what she knew to be the facts. 'And then what?' The words were still soft, her voice box bowled over by sensual needs, but there was strength in the words too, courage and willingness.

'And then what?' he repeated, the hands on her thighs moving the fabric a little, so his fingertips brushed the flesh at the top of her legs. She trembled in response, a thousand waves rocking through her.

Thought became a distant possibility, an island far out at sea. But she had to cling to it—every instinct she possessed was telling her she'd drown if she didn't. This was Santos Anastakos—a playboy! Way out of her league in every way and used to women falling at his feet. Did she really want to become just another notch on his bedpost? 'And then you'd have made me coffee the next morning, sent me away?' She couldn't quite summon a smile. 'And forgotten my name?'

His head snapped up, his eyes narrowing. Looking at him properly, she could see the rough hewing in and out of his chest as he dragged in breaths—he was as affected by this as she was, as completely at risk of drowning, despite his considerable experience.

'Why do you say that?'

'You think I didn't look you up on the internet?' She was trembling all over. Her body had never been at war with her mind before and now they were poles apart. She was having a visceral reaction to the idea of stepping backward, but mentally she was already distancing herself from him and the tension that pulled at her belly when they were near each other.

His eyes became guarded, his features an impenetrable mask. 'And what did the Internet have to say about me?'

Heat flushed her entire body. 'That you make love to a lot of women.' She dropped her gaze. 'That you have a habit of breaking hearts.'

'Breaking hearts?' He repeated the words with an emotional resonance that wasn't exactly amusement; if anything, it was more like shock. 'Amelia, believe me, I don't break anyone's heart. No one's *heart*—' he said the word with disdain '—is involved. The women I'm with know exactly what I want from them before anything happens.' His eyes scrutinised her face. 'Do you think I would have broken *your* heart?'

'No, of course not,' she denied immediately. 'But I'm nothing like you think. I'm nothing like Maria.'

'I know that,' he conceded swiftly, a frown furrowing his brow.

'I'm not someone who just sleeps with men.' She wished the words didn't sound so prudish! So disapproving! She wasn't. If anything, she was jealous of all the normal sexual exploration teens engaged in, the comfortable getting to know one's body—and other people's bodies—all the while learning what incites pleasure and enjoyment. She wished she'd had that experience, but nothing about her life had been normal. Her academic abillity had been endlessly isolating, then her parents cutting her from their life had further isolated her—she was, and had been for a long time, all alone.

'And you've had your heart broken before,' he guessed bitterly.

She had, but not in a romantic sense. No, it had been her parents, again and again; it had been the realisation as a teenager that their love for her was intrinsically tied to her academic achievements, her rare brilliance the only quality of hers they cared for, and particularly how it benefited them. She would never forget how they'd reacted on the day she'd told them she was leaving the International Agency of Space Exploration to become a teacher.

She pushed those thoughts aside. Even in that moment the things her parents had said to her, their threats and anger, had the power to hurt. It had been a valuable lesson, one Amelia would always remember: even people who claimed to love you could turn on a dime. No one was safe—love was fickle.

Santos was looking at her as though waiting for an answer. She considered his question and finally shook her head. He was asking about romantic pain, and with that she was a stranger.

'Never.' Awkwardness made her want to run from this but something ancient and almost magical stirred between them, pulling a semblance of truth from her.

'I don't have enough experience with men to have been hurt by them.' Her smile was a little haunted by the direction of her thoughts.

She felt him grow still, his eyes roaming her face, but he didn't say anything. Silence stretched between them, speculative and analytical. 'Let me guess: you're a romantic.' He said the words like an accusation, as though being romantically inclined was the worst thing in the world.

'I'm careful where I invest my energy,' she corrected. 'I can't be bothered to spend time with men who don't interest me. I don't like pretence. And I don't particularly like the risks that come from indiscriminate sex.'

'Risks?' The word was said with rich disbelief.

'Risks.' She nodded. 'Like getting pregnant and being left to raise a child completely on one's own. Like Cynthia,' she added, though it wasn't necessary. It was obvious from his features that her words had hit their mark. 'Is that what you meant by saying you've never broken anyone's heart? Because I think Cameron is an exception to that.'

Amelia wished she hadn't said the words as soon as they'd left her mouth. They were totally harsh and unreasonable, words that had come from a place of fear and uncertainty, words her brain had issued to put her body on notice. She closed her eyes, pain lancing her, regret making her face crumple.

'I didn't know about Cameron,' he said, but the words showed his own pain, his own hurt, and that made everything worse. 'If I had…'

'You didn't stay in touch with her?' Amelia prompted

more gently, but nothing could remove the sting from the question.

'No. It wasn't like that.' When he swallowed, his Adam's apple moved and her eyes were drawn to that motion. 'We spent a few nights together. We used protection. Neither of us wanted…ramifications. We discussed it enough to know that.'

'It's none of my business,' Amelia said stiffly, wishing she hadn't opened this can of worms. She forced her legs to obey her mental commands now, taking a small step backward, just as she had in his office. 'I only meant…' The words tapered off into nothing, but he nodded brusquely.

'I understood your meaning.' He spoke as though they were in the midst of negotiating a business deal. 'You think I go around screwing whoever I want and that secret love children are a likely result of my irresponsible life choices? You think there are a dozen Cynthias out there, a dozen Camerons, and that I'm wilfully ignoring my parental responsibilities in pursuit of the next night of hot sex?' He moved his face a little closer to hers so she saw the specks of silver in his ocean-grey eyes. 'You think I wouldn't have given everything I owned ten times over to know I had fathered a son? You think there's any version of reality in which I wouldn't have chosen to be a part of Cameron's life?'

Hot tears stung Amelia's eyes. 'I didn't mean…'

He lifted a finger to her lips, silencing her. 'Yes, you did. You're wrong about me, but it's what you think. Have the courage of your convictions, Amelia.'

'I don't… I just…' She was babbling. She shook her head and now she did what she'd wanted to do earlier, lifting a hand to his chest, pressing her fingers there urgently.

'You think if we'd had sex you might have ended up pregnant and that I would have abandoned you? You think that's what happened to Cynthia? I am shocked that she didn't even try to tell me I was a father. At no point—that I know of—did she so much as pick up her phone to tell me about our son. Not when she learned of her pregnancy, not when she had the boy, never. He'd never even heard of me.'

'Perhaps she thought you were already onto your next conquest?'

'And so what if I was?' The words were said softly but there was a deathly darkness to them. 'We weren't romantically involved. We had sex. If I was with someone else after her, that does nothing to alter the fact that I'd fathered a child. I would have supported her, supported him.' The words swirled around them, laced with regret. 'And if she hadn't died, Amelia? Do you think I would ever have learned the truth about him?'

Amelia's heart splintered at that question, because he was right—while Cynthia had done the responsible thing and put Santos's name in her will, it was clear that she'd had no intention of involving Cameron's father in their lives for as long as she lived.

'I have no idea how she conceived Cameron. It never occurred to me that she might have. I was younger, stupid in some ways, arrogant—but even then I always took measures to prevent unplanned consequences. She knew who I was and how to contact me. She should have told me about him.'

'Yes,' Amelia whispered. On that, they were in total agreement.

'I don't take risks. I don't get women pregnant and go into hiding.' He drew himself to his full height, stepping back from her, and his eyes glittered with such a cold ruthlessness that she shivered. 'And I would never have taken that risk with you.'

She swept her eyes shut because his words were completely unnecessary. She felt the truth in his soul. For a scientist, it was the least scientific thought she'd ever had. Then again, her education hadn't been limited to physics. She'd studied the Classics too, ancient Greek philosophers, Shakespeare and Jonson; she'd studied words that had helped her make sense of feelings and right now that education was pushing to the fore.

Desire was sweeping through her, refusing to be silenced. She'd fought it from the moment she'd met him, but now she wondered *why* she was bothering. She hadn't chosen to keep hold of her virginity. It wasn't as if she attached any special significance to it. She'd just never met a man who inspired her interest—until now. So what was she hesitating for? It wasn't as though Santos was offering any kind of complicated affair. He'd made it abundantly clear he wasn't into relationships. This was almost too good to be true—a chance to sleep with someone sophisticated and experienced who wouldn't want anything more from her. It was just the kind of no-strings arrangement that would rid her of her virginity, and introduce her to the world of sex without the necessity of emotional expectations.

'I was surprised by how much I wanted you,' she said simply, lifting a finger and tracing his lip in wonderment, the touch so simple but also so utterly sensual. 'The truth is, another minute and I'd have been begging you to kiss me to…make love…to me.' She stumbled a little over the words she'd never spoken before in reference to herself. 'Regardless of who was in the next room and in spite of the fact we'd just met. That's why I left so abruptly—because, honestly, that scared me.'

He inclined his head a little, his eyes beaming through her. 'And now?' The words were gravelled and heavily accented. Her heart rabbited inside her chest.

'And now,' she repeated, lost in thought. His eyes hooked to hers and he lifted his hands slowly, pushing the dress higher so he could slide his hands into the waistband of her underwear. She fluttered her eyes shut, breathing in deeply.

'Are you scared now?'

'Terrified,' she admitted with a tremor.

'Of me?' His thumb padded over the flesh of her lower back. She looked up at him then, meeting his gaze.

'That this will turn out to be just another dream.'

CHAPTER SIX

HE KISSED HER before he could second-guess his intentions, before she could even realise what he was doing. He crashed his mouth to hers, lacing their fingers together behind her back, dragging her towards him, his tongue sliding into her mouth at first in a slow exploration and then a cataclysmically urgent conquest. He groaned against her mouth, deepening the kiss, ignoring the persistent voice in the back of his head telling him there were a thousand reasons he should have the common sense to resist her.

'God, Santos.' She tore her fingers through his hair, her kiss laced with hunger, and he responded in kind, pushing her underpants aside so he could brush his fingers over her sex, teasing her there as he kissed her so hard her head pressed to the wall. She whimpered in his mouth, whispered his name, the words disjointed by passion; and, right as he felt her tremors build up to an almighty crash, he pushed a finger inside her, relishing the sensation of her muscles, their tight spasms almost bringing him to his own deafening crescendo. *Christos.* He felt like a schoolboy again, incapable of even a shred of control.

Despite what he'd just told her, he didn't actually make a habit of carrying condoms around his home. 'We need to take this to my bedroom.'

Her eyes widened. 'Through the house?'

He understood her hesitation. It was still early, but Chloe was probably awake. Leo too. 'You're right. Bad idea.' He looked over his shoulder towards the pool house. Carrying Amelia wrapped around his waist, striding quickly, he shouldered open the door, placing her on the day bed in the middle of the room.

She looked so completely bemused and sexy, lying there with her dress hitched around her waist, that he despised the necessity of leaving her even for a minutes.

'Stay here.' The words were unintentionally curt. He softened them with a smile, though he suspected it too came out terse. 'I'll be right back.'

He moved through the house quickly, retrieving protection from his bedside table and stalking back through the lounge area onto the terrace. He had escaped being seen and he'd never been more glad of anything in his life.

He wanted to have sex with Amelia more than he'd ever wanted another woman. It made no sense, but a part of him wondered if his fascination with her would dull once they slept together.

She was sitting up when he returned, and when he strode in her eyes were awash with feeling. *Christos*, she'd changed her mind. He braced for it, staring at her, waiting for her to tell him to stop.

She stood up and walked towards him; he held his breath. 'Well?'

Relief had him expelling all his breath in a rush, then

grinning. His response was to kiss her, and at the same time to lift her dress from her body, pulling their lips apart for the shortest possible time, just long enough to drive it over her head... And then he was back, kissing her, running his hands over her soft skin, swiftly unclasping her bra, letting it drop to the floor so he could fully palm her beautiful breasts in his hands, no cotton in the way. She was slender, but her breasts were rounded, the perfect size for his hands. He felt their weight, delighted in the puckering of her nipples, the goose bumps that teased her skin. He lifted her again, feeling her legs around his waist, almost the most pleasurable thing he'd ever known.

He fell to the bed with her, his weight on top of hers, his kisses trailing down her body now, his mouth driven to taste every square inch of her. When he took each of her nipples into his mouth, she cried out frantically, throwing her head from side to side, her voice high-pitched, her cries reverberating around the pool house.

Her need for him was obvious and he was surprised by the strength of his own desires; they were tearing through him, demanding response. On the one hand he wanted to savour this, to delight in the feeling of teasing her, but on the other he just wanted to bury himself inside her. Just like the first time they'd kissed when despite the imperfection of that moment—the timing, the location—he had been desperate for her in a way that had driven all sense from his head. It was a miracle he remembered to draw the condom over his erection, his hardness aching at the touch, so desperate was he to fill her around him.

'Christos.' He buried his face in the space above her

shoulder, his lips against the curtain of her dark hair, his breathing spasmodic. On autopilot he pushed his clothes from his body, impatience making his fingers catch in his zipper so that he cursed and then laughed unevenly. She was steadfastly watching him, her expression incomprehensible, her eyes fevered, her lips parted in a husky, silent invitation he couldn't ignore. He kissed her, the weight of his desperation pressing her head back to the mattress and into its softness, his hands roaming her body, parting her legs so he could wedge himself between her. The tip of his arousal brushed her womanhood and he groaned, the anticipation of what this would feel like making his blood zip and hum.

'Please!' She arched her back, rolling her hips in an ancient, primitive invitation that he had no intention of ignoring. Another time, he might have drawn this out, teased her desire to an even greater fever pitch, but his own needs were there, making that impossible.

'Yes,' he agreed, the word simple, his arousal pushing between her legs. He had wanted her almost the first moment he saw her and that desire had only increased with every day that had since passed, so now that he was on top of her, poised to take her, he had no patience for a gentle coming together. He drove himself into her, releasing a guttural cry as impossibly tight muscles almost tormented him, almost rejected him. Beneath him her body stiffened and the tightness inside her gave way, the feeling unfamiliar to him at first, so he pushed up on his elbows to stare at her, a frown on his face. She was looking at him, her skin pale, her eyes not meeting his.

It couldn't be... 'Amelia?' he demanded, knowing he should pull out of her but unable to make his body obey his brain's commands just yet.

Her eyes, frustratingly, were shielded from his. He pressed a finger beneath her chin, wondering at the different emotional responses that were pounding him from the inside—a sense of betrayal chief amongst them, but even that wasn't enough to dwarf the still-present longing for her.

'Amelia?'

But colour was returning to her cheeks and she was moving her hips now, arching her back, his erection buried inside her, her own needs obvious. He watched her for a second and then groaned because, whether she'd been a virgin or not, she definitely wasn't now, and desire was still threatening to engulf them.

He shifted his weight, pulling out of her a little so she lifted up higher, her eyes finding his at last. 'Don't stop.'

He was rarely surprised by anyone or anything but he was surprised now—and furious at himself for being so unable to read her. Looking back, there were myriad signs of her innocence, but he'd been too swept up in his own physical attraction to her. No; it wasn't just that. She was a woman in her twenties—a schoolteacher, for Christ's sake—why in the world would he assume she was a virgin?

How was that even possible?

'We need to talk about this.' The words were grunted from between snatched breaths—all that his raging blood made possible.

'Later,' she insisted, still moving her hips, so he

made a noise of acquiescence and dropped his mouth to hers, kissing her once more, pulling out of her slowly and easing himself back into her depths; trying with all his might to be gentle and to avoid hurting her when he wanted to take her with all his strength. It commanded every shred of willpower he possessed, but he held himself back, making love to her in a way that was only a fraction of his usual intensity; needing her to enjoy her first time, constantly needing to remind himself that she wasn't like him at all—this was all new to her.

Her muscles began to spasm around him, squeezing him hard, releasing then squeezing again, and her voice grew higher in pitch until she was saying his name over and over, the richness of his name in her plum British accent something he could listen to for ever. Later he would make her scream his name, when he took her just as he wanted, but for now…

The thought hit him from left field. *Later? For now?* There could be no 'later'. She was a virgin. This was her first time having sex. Hell, for all he knew she was imagining this to be the beginning of something longer term, and he didn't *do* longer term. But she knew that, didn't she? So why the hell was she having sex with him now?

Frustration gnawed at his belly. Santos hated not having all the answers almost as much as he hated surprises and today she'd made him feel both. She'd also made him feel as though he were floating through heaven on a cloud but that didn't matter. She'd lied to him. Not directly, but by omission; he wanted an explanation, and he swore to himself he'd get one.

* * *

'Well,' she said quietly when their breathing was more like normal. His weight on top of her was unexpectedly blissful, the roughness of his chest, his hairs there, pressing to her soft contours a new level of eroticism. Everything about this had been unexpected. She hadn't spent much time thinking about sex. It wasn't as though she'd had a reason to give it much consideration, having never really desired a man before. She understood the science behind it, and she'd obviously read books and seen films that featured sexual relationships, but nothing had prepared her for this.

Nothing.

Her body felt as though it had been pulled apart piece by piece and then reshaped gently, lovingly, into a whole new being. She sighed softly, stretched a little then stopped when the very movement threatened to dislodge him from her—she didn't want that.

When he lifted his head above hers, though, his expression was like ice. His cheeks were still slashed with dark colour, the way they had been when passion had filled his veins, but his features were now trained into a mask of cool inquisition. 'You were a virgin.'

It wasn't a question so much as a statement. An accusation. She swallowed hard, a small frown forming a divot between her brows.

'Yes.' There was no sense in lying.

He nodded stiffly then shifted, pulling away from her so she was tempted to reach for him and draw him back. Only, when he stood, his spine, was ramrod-straight, tension emanating from him with every step he took. She watched as he strode across the room, disappearing for a few seconds before returning with a towel slung low around his hips, his eyes boring into her from across the room.

Feeling at a distinct disadvantage, she sat up and reached for the closest thing she could find, a blanket that was loose at the foot of the bed. She wrapped it around her shoulders and somehow managed to speak calmly when she next addressed him. 'And you're annoyed about that?'

Perturbation expressed itself in the flattening of his lips. 'I don't give a damn about your sexual history except for one point, Amelia. I don't sleep with virgins.'

'That feels like a form of sexual discrimination.' She attempted a joke, but it fell flat. His mood was positively arctic and a shiver ran down her spine. Something like a stitch was gripping her heart, but a thousand times more painful than any she'd ever known.

'I don't want to date you.' The words were like a whip on her spine. 'I'm not interested in a relationship—with you or anyone. I'm the last man in the world you should have given your virginity to.'

The antiquated turn of phrase had her feminist hackles rising. 'I didn't "give" you anything,' she snapped, then made an effort to grab hold of her temper. 'We had sex—and you might not have known I was a virgin but I did.'

'Exactly,' he retorted decisively. 'You knew and I should have known. You should have let me decide if I wanted to be your first lover.'

'You make it sound like some great chore.'

'It is a responsibility and it can bring with it expectations. *Christos*, Amelia, what were you thinking?'

The truth was, she hadn't been thinking. It hadn't really occurred to her that he might notice, let alone mind. 'I just...'

But he was furious and it showed. 'Do not make the mistake of thinking this means anything.' He slashed his hand through the air. 'Nothing about this changes what I wanted from you when we came in here.'

His words were cutting—deliberately so, she suspected—as though he was looking to hurt her as a way of demonstrating how ill-suited he was to be her first lover. How disinclined to offer any kind of tenderness.

And his assumption had her temper bursting through her, its ferocity a relief from the throbbing ache that was spreading in her blood—not a physical pain so much as one born of rejection and hurt. She'd known both those feelings often enough to recognise them now, and she knew that refuge lay in her temper, so she armed herself with it gladly, fixing him with a glare she hoped would pass for impatience.

'You wanted to make love to me,' she said darkly.

'I wanted to have sex with you,' he corrected.

She almost rolled her eyes. 'And now that we've had sex you think I'm going to fall in love with you? Are you actually standing over there all terrified that I'm waiting for a proposal or something? Geez, Santos, I don't have much experience with men but I'm twenty-four years old—I have a fair idea of how the world works.'

And now she gave into temptation and rolled her eyes, pushing off the bed while carefully keeping her blanket tucked around her shoulders. Her dress and underwear were in opposite directions. She prioritised her dress, scooping it off the floor then turning her back on him while she dragged it over her head, dropping the blanket as the dress fell into place before whirling around to find him staring at her with a small frown on his face.

He opened his mouth, about to say something, but she cut him off. 'I wanted what you wanted. To have sex. And now I want nothing to do with you.' Her glare was only slightly reduced in effect by the suspiciously moist layer over her eyes.

She held his gaze for two long seconds and then began to stride towards the door; she'd come back to find her underwear later. But when she was almost at the door he was galvanised into action, his fingers curling around her wrist, spinning her round and holding her still.

'Damn it, Amelia, that's not—'

'What?' A single tear slid down her cheek and she ground her teeth.

Hold it together.

'I was anything but gentle with you. If I had known it was your first time—'

'Then you'd have never slept with me,' she snapped.

His eyes narrowed, his chest pushing out with the force of his breath. 'So you chose not to tell me?'

'I—no. I wasn't thinking clearly.'

'Damn straight. Did it occur to you that I wouldn't want this—to be your first lover? Did it occur to you that I prefer to sleep with women who know what sex is all about?'

Hurt and mortification contorted her features. She angled her face away and when she answered him it was in a voice that was rich with hurt. 'It didn't occur to me that you'd notice. Or mind.'

His laugh lacked humour. 'I've been with enough women to know the difference.' She doubted he meant the words to hurt but they did. Her insides were still trembling with the force of his possession, pleasure still receding, and he was reminding her of how many conquests he'd had?

'Yes, well, I was a virgin. I'm sorry you were disappointed, or whatever, but that wasn't my intention.' She yanked her wrist out of his grip, covering the slightly pink flesh with her fingertips, but not before his eyes had dropped to her wrist and observed the small marks there.

'Before I came here you told me I'd barely see you,' she said stiffly, moving to the door of the pool house. 'I hope you honour that promise.' Tilting her chin away from him, she turned her back and walked past the pool—even when she felt like running—and into the house. The sun had risen over Agrios Nisi but it breathed no light into Amelia.

He wasn't conscious of how long he stayed in the pool house. He dressed slowly, his mind ticking over what had just happened. Something caught his eye; he reached down and lifted her underwear off the floor, stuffing it in his pocket. Knowing it was there sent something spiralling through him—an urgent wave of need that hadn't been alleviated by their coming together.

How had she thought her virginity wouldn't matter to him? Why hadn't she realised it was something a man would want to know before having sex with a woman?

He stood at the foot of the bed, staring at it before sweeping his eyes closed and seeing Amelia—seeing her as she'd been in the throes of passion, and then in anguish afterwards, as he'd separated from her and hurled accusations at her until her eyes had gleamed and tears had moistened her beautiful, expressive eyes.

Christos.

The idea of being in a relationship with a woman was anathema to him and always had been. Not once had he questioned that. His father was blithely unaware of the true cost of his constant pursuit of 'love', but Santos wasn't. Santos had seen the emotional consequences first hand—initially with his mother, who'd had to be hospitalised for severe depression after the divorce, and then in Nico's subsequent wives. Each of them had suffered at the hands of his father and Santos had promised he would never be like him.

He enjoyed the company of women, and he loved sex, but sex was easy to control—it was an exchange, no different from the kind of commercially motivated deals he made every day. True, there was no exchange of money, just satisfaction, but the parameters were as inviolable as if a contract had been formed. Santos offered a good time in bed. Full stop. The end. There were no gifts, no promises, no damned romance that went beyond a drink in a bar, and only then as a precursor to a night of passion.

He didn't swap life stories with these women but on some level, he was always careful. Finely honed business skills served him well in his private life; it was impossible to switch those traits off. He never slept with a woman who didn't fit the mould he sought—a woman who was sophisticated and experienced, who understood what he wanted and was happy to oblige. He was, ordinarily, painfully careful to not take any woman to bed who didn't share his view on relationships.

A virgin? *Christos.* Even with what Amelia had said, the derisive way she'd scoffed at the very idea of waiting for a marriage proposal, it didn't change the fact that someone's virginity should *mean* something. Her first time should have involved more than a quick lay in the pool house, for God's sake. Surely she could see that? So why the hell had she come here with him? Why hadn't she told him, so he could at least have been gentle with her?

He ground his teeth together, all the 'what ifs' in the world not changing the facts.

He'd slept with her; he was her first lover. And he'd hurt her. Not physically, necessarily—though, hell, he'd taken no effort to ease her into it; he'd simply driven into her, removing the barrier of her innocence and making her completely his.

More than that, he'd hurt her with his behaviour afterwards. He'd been angry and, though he'd had every right to feel that, he should have exercised more control, keeping a grip on his feelings in deference to hers.

He hadn't. He'd said everything he'd thought and witnessed the ramifications of that. The way she'd looked away from him when he'd told her he was used to lovers who knew what sex was about! Talk about offensive and insensitive.

He closed his eyes and inhaled deeply; the room smelled like her.

Thialo. He'd *hurt* her. Amelia had been wrong not to tell him the truth, but she was still Amelia. Kind, generous Amelia who'd come to his house to beg him to be a better father to Cameron. And she deserved better than this—his mistreatment and now his disdain. With a dip of his head he moved out of the cabana, cutting across the terrace and moving through the house, taking the steps two at a time.

He knocked on her bedroom door; there was no answer. He hesitated only a moment, figuring he'd already crossed a line with her, before pushing into her room. It was empty. A second later he heard the shower running and something punched at his gut: it was as if she couldn't wait to wash him off her.

That stoked his masculine pride. If he'd been less in control of his impulses he might have pulled the shower door open and joined her, whispering against her flesh that he wanted to show her what her first time should have been like.

He didn't.

Instead, he sat on the edge of the bed and he waited. He hated that he'd hurt her, but not because Amelia meant anything to him. This was his own code of honour, one he'd sworn to uphold, and for the first time in his adult life he'd done something that didn't sit well within the bounds of that. He'd fix it, and then move on.

Easy.

CHAPTER SEVEN

'OH, MY GOD, Santos!' She stared at him, her heart pounding in her throat, her eyes huge as she regarded him across the room. He was dressed as he had been that morning, but it was impossible to see him without seeing *all* of him now. She refused to think about him naked, refused to think about how he'd felt on top of her, inside her. 'You scared me half to death!' She was pleased when the exclamation emerged with a degree of irritation.

'We weren't finished talking.' The words were quiet, carefully blanked of emotion, which was reassuring. Dressed in only a fluffy robe, she felt at a disadvantage, but she had no intention of showing him that. She moved towards the window—a safe distance away from where he sat on the edge of the bed—and planted her bottom on the window's ledge.

'I'm not sure there's anything else to talk about,' she muttered, lifting her shoulders as she dropped her gaze to the thick carpet.

'I was angry.' The words were simple and unexpected.

'No kidding.'

'I should have realised the difference in our experience but, the truth is, the intensity of my own needs for you deafened me to anything else.' His grimace was wry, and then he stood, moving towards her so she had only a few seconds in which to brace, to fortify herself against her body's instinctive reaction.

'I hurt you.'

She blinked, her heart turning over in her chest. Had she been so easy to read?

'I wasn't gentle, and I would have been if I'd known. I would have made it so much better for you.' He expelled a breath, his eyes heavy on her face. 'Your first time shouldn't be rushed like that. It should have been special, different.'

She didn't admit that it had felt damned special to her—until his anger and disappointment had become evident.

'It was fine,' she said simply, turning her face away, no longer wanting to look at him, aware of how easily he could read her features.

'"Fine" has never been a benchmark I considered worth aiming for.'

Her stomach squeezed. 'It was better than fine. Is that what you want to hear? Did you come here for praise, Santos? To hear that you were *amazing*?'

Out of her peripheral vision she saw him shake his head and then he was crouching before her, his hand on her knee gentle and so kind that it was somehow all the worse. She resolutely straightened her spine, refusing to show him any more overt sentimentality.

'I came here to apologise.'

It shocked her. She swivelled to face him, biting down on her lower lip. 'I was angry that you would choose me to be your first lover, because of all the things I cannot offer you, but I shouldn't have spoken to you the way I did. I don't want that to be your memory of losing your virginity.'

She nodded a little awkwardly. 'I'm not—I wasn't building it up to be some big, momentous event.' She cleared her throat. 'It's not like I was "saving myself" or anything so quaint.'

He pounced on her denial. 'So how does it happen then that a beautiful woman in her twenties had never had sex?'

'I just hadn't.' She pulled away from him, standing, turning a little to look out of the window. The Aegean glistened beneath her, beautiful and expansive, bright and blue.

'There has to be more to it.'

'Why?' She angled her face to his. 'Why can't it be something I just never got around to?'

'Because you are a sensual woman, and to have not indulged that side of your nature makes no sense.'

She nodded, his confusion easy to understand. 'It's a long story and I'm not sure it really matters.'

'I don't like mysteries.'

Her laugh was involuntary, a small sound of disbelief. 'Is that what I am?'

He didn't answer.

'I'm sorry I didn't tell you,' she said honestly. 'I wondered if I should but then once we were in the pool house I couldn't really think of anything except—'

'Except?' He moved a little closer, his face almost touching hers.

She swallowed. 'What we were doing.' She turned back to the window, needing some mental space from him.

He stood beside her for several beats, and a thousand thoughts and feelings rammed into her brain, asking to be spoken, but she stayed quiet, staring out to sea.

'Please let me know if you need anything,' he said a little formally, taking a step back from her. 'If I did hurt you, and you need—'

She shook her head in frustration. 'I'm not made of glass, Santos.'

'I'm aware of that.'

'Are you?' She regarded him carefully, her stomach in knots. There were many things about her life she might have changed if she could but she'd never wished more keenly to reach back through the fabric of time and alter her social experiences. She was aware how out of kilter she was much of the time—an anomaly— yet she'd learned to cover that, to integrate for the most part. But with Santos she felt like all her usual defences were missing; she was vulnerable and raw.

'I am sorry.'

'Stop saying that.' She brushed his apology aside. 'I get that you wish it hadn't happened, that you wouldn't have slept with me if you'd known I hadn't done that before, but *I knew* and I chose to have sex with you and I'm still happy with that decision.' She realised, as she said it, that it was true. 'I'm glad we had sex. I liked being with you. I'm sorry if that's disrespecting your wishes but I need to say it so you can stop tormenting yourself.'

She didn't let him speak. 'I'm not secretly imagining changing my name to Amelia Anastakos. I'm not fantasising about waking up beside you every morning for the rest of the time I'm on Agrios Nisi. I'm a big girl, Santos. As you keep pointing out, I'm in my twenties, and I understand how men like you operate. Sex is sex, and I'm more than okay with that.'

He stared at her, the words wrapping around him, each of them perfectly chosen to relax him, a balm to his worries. She was letting him off the hook, making him understand that she'd gone into this with her eyes wide open. His only objection, the root of his anger, was his fear that he had unknowingly hurt her—that perhaps he'd led her on in some way, that she'd chosen to give him her virginity because she'd been hoping it might lead to something bigger, but she was telling him clearly that wasn't the case.

She'd wanted to have sex. That was all. It was no big deal. Meaningless, temporary, perfect.

So why didn't he feel better? Why hadn't her words done a bit to relax him? Why were they having almost the opposite effect?

I understand how men like you operate.

Men like him? Men like his father, did she mean? It coated the inside of his mouth with acid. He was nothing like Nico Anastakos. He'd spent a lifetime proving that.

'You should not have let me be your first. I cannot give you—'

'God, Santos!' She laughed, shaking her head. 'I just told you, you don't have to *give* me anything. I don't know what it is with you. I've never met anyone that I looked at and felt…'

Her words tapered off. What had she been about to say? *Felt like I wanted to rip their clothes from their body?*

She closed her eyes on a wave of embarrassment.

'It shouldn't have happened.' When he sighed, his breath fanned her temple, warm and distracting. She angled her face away.

'You don't have to worry. It definitely won't happen again.'

One of his stepmothers had bought him a puppy—a little brown Labrador. Santos had named it Atrómitos—Atró for short. He'd been ten, and it had been very easy to love the dog. Hard to lose it when the inevitable separation occurred and his temporary stepmother decided to take Atró away with her.

During thunderstorms Atró had cried, and the noise Santos heard in the early hours of the morning was so reminiscent of that sound he thought he was slipping back in time. He pushed up in his bed, his heart pounding, disorientation making him frown, and then he moved as the reality of what was happening woke him fully.

'Cameron.' He didn't pause to pull on a shirt. Striding from his bedroom in only a pair of boxers, he moved through his home towards the suite of rooms he'd assigned his son. The cries grew louder as he approached. He pushed open the door and then paused.

His son was crying, but he wasn't alone. Amelia was beside him in the bed, her arms wrapped around him, her hair like burnt caramel in the soft light of his room. He hadn't seen her in days—not since he'd left her room with an uneasiness in his gut that she was casting him in the same light as his father—and for a moment all he could do was stare. Her elegant fingers moved over Cameron's head, brushing the curls away from his temples, her words too soft for Santos to catch. Her pyjamas were hardly intended to seduce—a T-shirt and a loose pair of pants—but, knowing her body as he now did, it didn't matter how she chose to dress herself. His reaction was instant—a stirring in his blood, a question his body wanted answered.

After a slight delay, she appeared to notice him, moving her eyes towards the door, her lips compressing, casting her face in an expression he didn't understood.

He forced himself to look away from Amelia. *Christos*, he found that harder than he cared to admit. His son's little face was streaked with tears, his eyes bloodshot, his small body moving with the violent force of his sobs.

'Can I…?' Frustration bit through him. He wasn't used to this—not knowing what to say, how to act. He'd felt like this ever since he'd found out about Cameron. He hated it.

Amelia almost felt sorry for him. His uncertainty was patently obvious. How could he see his son in such obvious distress and not simply rush into the room and bundle him into a reassuring hug? Perhaps he would have if Amelia hadn't reached him first. Perhaps it was her being here that was confusing him.

She grimaced, turning her attention back to Cameron, very close to wishing that it had all never happened. Even as she thought it, she pushed the very idea away. She'd never regret what they'd shared.

'There, there,' she murmured, stroking the darling boy's hair, brushing her lips over his brow. 'I'm here, darling.'

'I just...' His little voice was so sad, and Amelia's heart ached for him. 'I miss her so much.'

'Of course you do,' she agreed, catching one of his hands and squeezing it.

Without intending it, her eyes moved to the door. Santos was blocking it. The light cast from the lamp was faint and golden, shading his face in a collection of geometric shadows.

'Would you get Cameron a drink of water?' she suggested quietly.

'Water, *nai*.' His voice did funny things to her stomach. He moved quickly, turning and leaving, relieved to have something to do.

Amelia kept talking to Cameron, reminding him of all that she knew about Cynthia and of England; of the first day they'd met—short little anecdotes that seemed to work. When she made intentional little mistakes, Cameron, in that way children had, effortlessly corrected her. 'No, I wasn't wearing a red shirt, because we were dressed in house colours; it must have been blue.'

Santos didn't take long, striding across the room. She looked in his general direction rather than towards the wall of muscles that was right at her side.

'Thank you.' She held the glass out to Cameron. He'd stopped crying now, though his breaths were shallow. He drank half and then Amelia stood, almost bumping into Santos—she would have done so had he not moved quickly, sidestepping her with easy athleticism. She placed the water on the bedside table and rearranged an exhausted Cameron, easing him back against the pillows, his little face dark in contrast to the crisp white pillows, stroking his hair until his eyes grew heavy.

'Amelia?'

His voice was thick with tiredness.

'Yes, dearest?'

'I'm glad you're here.'

Her heart flipped over in her chest. She straightened, watching as sleep devoured him, turning his breathing rhythmic, relaxing his little face.

Santos moved behind her, surprising her, and she stiffened, bracing her body to ward off its usual, predictable, unwanted response to his proximity, but he was only turning off the lamp. The room plunged into darkness.

Amelia moved towards the door, aware he was right behind her, crossing into the corridor.

'What happened?' he asked, almost unnecessarily.

'He had a dream. About Cynthia.' There was a little light out here, coming from a room down the hallway. A quick glance showed the foot of a bed. Santos's room? Great. That was a detail she'd prefer not to know.

'He was so upset.'

'Well, yes,' Amelia agreed. 'He woke up thinking it had all been a terrible nightmare, that his mother was still here, only to realise he's living that nightmare.'

Santos's jaw clenched tight and Amelia could have kicked herself for being so insensitive.

'I don't mean that knowing you is a nightmare—'

'I know what you meant.' His eyes lingered on her face, so her heart skipped a beat.

'Anyway…' She let the word hang in the air. What was she waiting for? An invitation? How ridiculous.

'You're so comfortable with him.'

That pulled on her focus. She lifted a brow, but before he could say anything else he put a hand in the small of her back, guiding her a little way down the hallway, away from Cameron's bedroom.

'I'm a schoolteacher,' she said quietly. 'I spend my days with six-year-olds, and I've known Cam for years. It's easy for me to be comfortable with him.'

He nodded, but his eyes were still appraising her, distracting her, making it hard to concentrate. *What genius?* she thought with a self-deprecating grimace.

'You just need to spend time with him,' she urged quietly. 'Getting to know him will make you feel more comfortable.' She tilted her head to the side. 'You work such long hours. It's no wonder you don't feel comfortable with him yet. Why don't you take some time off? Or even truncate your work day a little so that you can have breakfast with him, or dinner? It takes time, Santos,' she pressed when he didn't say anything. 'There's no magic pill, no secret. Time and attention.'

His expression was like stone, reminding her of the first night here.

Do not expect miracles while you are here. Your concern is my son's happiness, not his relationship with me.

'Anyway,' she said again, on a small sigh. 'He's asleep now.'

'Nai.'

Neither of them moved. The air around them seemed to thicken, making breathing almost impossible. God, he must work out a lot to have a physique like this. Her eyes followed the ridges of his chest, chasing each undulation until her breath was burning inside her lungs and her fingertips were tingling with a desire to follow the course of her eyes.

She had to break free of him now or it would be too late. She stifled a groan but before she could turn and move away he lifted a hand and curved it over her cheek.

Neither of them spoke, but she felt a thousand and one things deep in her soul. 'I am very grateful you came here, Amelia.'

For Cameron, she mentally added. Of course, for Cameron.

She nodded, dislodging his hand, and took a step back while she still could. 'So am I.' Silence wrapped around them once more.

He broke it. '*Kalinychta*, Miss Ashford.'

'Goodnight, Santos.'

He couldn't say why but after Amelia had left him, disappearing into her own room, he didn't return to his own. He couldn't. Not while his son's cries were still at the uppermost of his mind. He had no idea what he could do to ease the young boy's suffering if he awoke again but he wanted to be there if grief tore through his sleep once more.

It was a long night but Santos didn't sleep. Instead, he sat beyond his son's door, crouched in the corridor, his head bent, his breathing deep, perched ready to react if Cameron needed him. He couldn't explain why, but in that moment, for that night, Santos obeyed one of his instincts—that to comfort his son.

The other instinct—to be wrapped up in Amelia Ashford and how he'd like them to spend their night— he ignored resolutely.

It's no wonder you don't feel comfortable with him yet. Why don't you take some time off? Or even truncate your work day a little so that you can have breakfast with him, or dinner? It takes time, Santos.

She was right. Of course she was right. He couldn't avoid the fact he was a father. He might not have any idea how to *be* a father but that didn't change the fact. And since when had Santos Anastakos been a man to run from the unfamiliar? Never. Whatever he'd faced in his business life, he had conquered, even when that meant scaling an almost impossible mountain.

This would be no different.

A week after Cameron's broken sleep, after he'd spent the night in a silent vigil outside his son's room, Santos surprised them all at dinner—Talia, Cameron and Amelia—even more so when he took a seat at the head of the table, accepting a plate of food and a wine glass from one of the helpers Chloe hired through the summer to keep on top of the housework.

He watched Amelia across the table as she spoke to Cameron and Talia, completely calm and reserved, no hint of emotion on her features, no hint of warmth at his presence. What had he expected? A marching band? For her to pause proceedings and congratulate him on doing something so banal as returning home a few hours earlier than normal?

'That can't be true!' Talia laughed but Amelia shook her head so her dark hair shifted around her face, distracting him with its glossy, water-like consistency, reminding him of the way it had tousled around her face when she'd been in the bed in the pool room.

'It absolutely is.'

'How can it be?' Cameron placed his cutlery neatly in the middle of his plate. Santos turned his attention to his son and as always felt the clip of pain—the gaping hole inside him where knowledge and familiarity should have been. Cameron had excellent manners—a credit to his mother, he supposed. He wished he could remember more about Cynthia. The truth was, he'd been twenty-seven and celebrating a huge takeover of a rival shipping company the night they'd met. He'd spent most of their time together either responding to emails or drinking Scotch.

'The warmth in the atmosphere causes a thermal expansion,' Amelia said with a smile. She lifted her knife, holding it in the air. 'When the weather gets warm, the iron that was used to build the Eiffel Tower grows bigger—expands—until it's around four inches taller than in winter.'

'I don't believe it!' Cameron laughed. 'It's a building, they can't change shape.'

'Not shape, necessarily, just size,' she insisted, laying her knife back down. 'When I was studying in Paris, we measured it over the course of the year.'

'You studied in Paris?' Santos's voice came out deep and Amelia's gaze flicked to him, something flashing in her eyes so it was impossible not to feel the snaking heat of response. It had been several days since he'd last seen her and when she looked at him now he wanted to stand up and drag her body to his, to throw her over his shoulder and carry her upstairs. He wanted to spend a long, hot night making love to her, rather than the rushed coming together they'd experienced in the pool house.

'Yes.' She lifted one perfect brow in a silent challenge then turned back to Cameron. It was as if she felt nothing for Santos, no temptation, no curiosity. Frustration shifted inside him—he wanted to kiss her until that ice dropped from her completely, until it melted away in an incontrovertible acknowledgement of desire.

'How did you measure it?'

'With lasers, of course.' She smiled and Santos tried to focus his thoughts; the strength of his erection beneath the table was hardly helpful.

He could see what a good teacher she'd be. She was patient and engaging and seemed genuinely passionate about the subject matter.

'But what—?'

'No more questions for Miss Ashford.' Talia grinned, standing up and resting her hands on the back of the chair. 'It's time for bed.'

'But it's only seven-thirty!'

'Exactly,' Talia said with a crisp nod. 'The perfect time for little boys to have their stories read.'

'I'm not tired.'

Amelia's smile was all indulgence. 'You always say that, right before your head hits the pillow and you're fast asleep within minutes.'

Something inside Santos shifted. Guilt? Jealousy? He had no idea about his son's bedtime rhythms.

Cameron opened his mouth to challenge that statement but then nodded with a glimmer of obedience. 'Okay, then.' He stood up and rounded the table, coming to Amelia's side. She lifted an arm around him, holding him there, burying her face in his hair, and for a minute there was such a look of unguarded sadness and love on her features that his breath snagged in his throat.

'Goodnight, darling.' She kissed his hair, smiling directly into his eyes. Warmth replaced the sadness; she was beautiful.

'Night.' Cameron moved further down the table. It was a new thing for Santos to dine with his son. Even in England, Santos had come home too late for Cameron's mealtime. They therefore didn't have any kind of routine established and the little boy looked unsure as to what to say or do to his father. It clutched something tight in Santos's chest.

He smiled reassuringly, his gut churning for how alike they were—Cameron could have been Santos at the same age. 'You know,' he said thoughtfully, scanning the little boy's face. 'Paris is only a short flight from here. Perhaps we could go there and see the magical, growing Eiffel Tower for ourselves?'

Cameron's eyes turned into little round plates of blue. 'Really?'

'Really.' He shifted his attention to Amelia. 'What do you think, Miss Ashford?'

She sat back in her seat as a young woman cleared the plates. 'I think Cameron would enjoy that,' Amelia said with a small smile, reserved just for the little boy.

'I would.'

Santos laughed. 'Then I'll arrange it.' He didn't expect his son to hug him. It was still new—they were learning. But he reached out and tousled Cameron's hair, then put his hand on his shoulder. *'Kalinychta.'*

Amelia's eyes flew to his, and now heat sparked between them. She wasn't ice. Not at all.

'What does that mean?'

'It means goodnight.'

'Kalinychta,' Cameron repeated, his pronunciation close to perfect.

'Excellent,' Santos praised.

'Kalinychta,' Cameron said again, apparently enjoying the feeling of the word in his mouth. He repeated it to Amelia as he left the room, Talia's arm wrapping around Cameron's shoulder as she shepherded him away for the night.

Leaving Santos alone with Amelia.

'Well.' She moved to stand, as though she couldn't leave quickly enough. He shook his head, the single gesture holding her where she was a moment. Their eyes held, a challenge moving from him to her and being returned with twice the intensity, so his whole body began to ache for her, to want her, to imagine what being with her would be like.

'When were you in Paris?'

She reached forward, toying with the stem of her wine glass. It was filled with a clear liquid—mineral water. 'I went last summer.' She sipped her drink.

'To measure the Eiffel Tower?'

'No, that was when I was a student.'

'A school exchange?'

She hesitated a moment, as if choosing her words

with care. 'No. I was enrolled at the Académie for a time.'

He couldn't say why he was surprised. Perhaps it was the idea of a teacher from a down-at-heel comprehensive school having studied at one of the most prestigious institutions of tertiary education in the world.

'What did you study?' He leaned back in his chair, reaching for his own glass—his filled with red wine from grapes that were grown here on the island.

Another hesitation. Was he imagining the blush on her cheeks? For what reason?

'Mathematics.'

He watched her as he took a drink of wine then replaced his glass on the table. 'That's your speciality?'

'I don't really have one speciality,' she said, obfuscating a little, and now she stood, fixing him with a cool gaze. 'I do, however, have work to do.'

'It will wait.'

Her expression clearly showed surprise. 'I beg your pardon?'

'Don't beg my pardon,' he responded, his eyes half-shuttered, his chest expanding with the strength of his need for her. 'Just sit back down and talk to me while I finish my dinner.'

'Mr Anastakos…'

'Amelia.' He laughed then, a thick, gruff sound. 'Do I need to remind you of how well we know one another?'

Her lips parted on a small noise of shock. The ice was gone. He wondered if she'd been like that for Cameron's benefit. Perhaps it was a defensive mechanism, so that no one else realised what had happened between them?

She shook her head a little warily. 'No.'

'So, please, call me Santos. And sit down.'

She stayed right where she was, staring at him, so frustration bubbled through him. He pushed his chair back, standing, moving to the chair at his right and drawing it from the table.

'Sit,' he instructed, his eyes mocking. 'I don't bite.'

He saw the way she swallowed, her hesitation making him want to pull her into the chair—better yet, onto his lap. He didn't. His desire for her was hard enough to control without bringing any physical contact into the equation. But he had to control it. Amelia was off-limits.

'Fine.' He stayed where he was as she sat down, pushing her chair in a little, resisting an impulse to brush her shoulders with his fingertips. She was wearing a simple dress with spaghetti straps, her bare skin flawless and golden. When they'd made love, his stubble had left red marks there. On her shoulders, above her breasts. How long had they stayed on her skin before fading into nothingness? And why could he think of little other than dragging his mouth over her body now, leaving the same trail of red marks, the same covering of goose bumps, over her skin?

'Cameron was very happy you came home for dinner.' She said the words with a slight hint of reproach and he understood her reasons for it. He wanted to tell her that he was new to all this, and to be patient with him. He wanted to tell her that he didn't know what

One Minute" Survey

You get up to **FOUR** books <u>and</u> TWO Mystery Gifts...

ABSOLUTELY FREE!

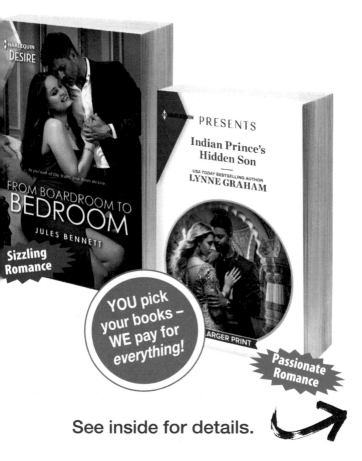

See inside for details.

Dear Reader,

Your opinions are important to us. So if you'll participate in our fa
and free "One Minute" Survey, **YOU** can pick up to four wonder
books that **WE** pay for!

As a leading publisher of women's fiction, we'd love to hear from
you. That's why we promise to reward you for completing our
survey.

IMPORTANT: Please complete the survey and return it. We'll ser
your Free Books and Free Mystery Gifts right away. **And we pay
for shipping and handling too!**   ← *We pay for*
                                      EVERYTHING!

Try **Harlequin® Desire** books featuring the worlds of the
American elite with juicy plot twists, delicious sensuality and
intriguing scandal.

Try **Harlequin Presents® Larger-Print** books featuring the
glamourous lives of royals and billionaires in a world of exotic
locations, where passion knows no bounds.

Or TRY BOTH!

Thank you again for participating in our "One Minute"
Survey. It really takes just a minute (or less) to complete the
survey… and your free books and gifts will be well worth it!

Sincerely,

Pam Powers

Pam Powers
for Reader Service

"One Minute" Survey

GET YOUR FREE BOOKS AND FREE GIFTS!

✓ Complete this Survey   ✓ Return this survey

1 Do you try to find time to read every day?

☐ YES   ☐ NO

2 Do you prefer stories with happy endings?

☐ YES   ☐ NO

3 Do you enjoy having books delivered to your home?

☐ YES   ☐ NO

4 Do you find a Larger Print size easier on your eyes?

☐ YES   ☐ NO

YES! I have completed the above "One Minute" Survey. Please send me my Free Books and Free Mystery Gifts (worth over $20 retail). I understand that I am under no obligation to buy anything, as explained on the back of this card.

☐ I prefer Harlequin® Desire 225/326 HDL GNWS

☐ I prefer Harlequin Presents® Larger Print 176 /376 HDL GNWS

☐ I prefer BOTH 225/326 & 176/376 HDL GNW4

FIRST NAME   LAST NAME

ADDRESS

APT.#   CITY

STATE/PROV.   ZIP/POSTAL CODE

the hell he was doing with the child, but that he wanted to work it out.

But Santos wasn't a man who generally bared his soul, so he said instead, 'And you, Amelia? Were you happy I came home for dinner?'

CHAPTER EIGHT

'I'M HAPPY YOU spent some time with your son.' She evidently chose the words with care, her manner crisp. He dipped his head forward, concealing a wolfish smile, before changing the subject.

'How long were you in Paris for?' He sat down in his own chair with a lithe athleticism, reminding her of some kind of wild predator, all strength and muscle.

'A little over a year.' Her mouth was dry but her water was finished.

'Would you like some wine?'

She eyed it for a moment before nodding. The moment he'd walked into the room she'd begun to tremble, her insides awash with fierce recognition, as though he were a magnet and she the perfect polar opposite.

When she was thirteen, she'd been badly bullied by a student at college. The girl was seventeen and should have known better but she'd made it her mission to make Amelia's life hell. Amelia had prided herself on not showing the bully how badly it hurt, nor how upset she'd been with the cruel name-calling. She'd perfected a calm exterior that rarely failed, even when her insides were being shredded to pieces. Her heart had been slamming into her ribs and her pulse filling her ears with a tsunami-like power but, outwardly at least, she'd kept calm.

With Santos, that had been almost impossible and tonight, the first time she'd seen him since they'd slept together, the effort had cost her. He'd strolled into the dining room, in the midst of their happy domesticity, and her body had begun to reverberate, as if recognising its master. She'd found it almost impossible not to look at him during dinner but she hadn't been able to look—not without staring. It had been a difficult forty minutes. Wine was welcome.

She watched as he poured the rich burgundy liquid into her glass, half-filling it.

'What is it?' She lifted it to her nose, inhaling its wooded fragrance.

'*Xinomavro.*' The word had an almost magical-sounding quality. 'A type of grape varietal that grows well on the island.'

'You grow it here?'

He made a noise of agreement. 'It ages well, so each harvest is bottled and stored for at least five years before it's sent to my homes around the world.'

She stared at him for several seconds and then laughed. 'I'm sorry, I know you're probably used to that, with your helicopter and jets and whatever else, but do you have idea how unusual what you just said is?'

His expression showed a hint of amusement. 'I do.'

She took a sip, her eyes roaming his face, the same flicker of need that had been tormenting her all week flaring to violent life. She'd felt it endlessly—need, desire, impatience and hunger. What they'd started had launched a thousand wants within her. At twenty-four she'd had her first sexual awakening and, far from satisfying her curiosity, it had only served to fill her with renewed curiosity.

'I can't imagine growing up with that kind of money,' she said honestly, thinking back to her own childhood, how marred it had been by intense poverty—how incredible the contrast when she'd started travelling and suddenly they'd been able to afford some non-essentials, and eventually even a few luxuries. As a child, she hadn't really connected her activities with an improvement in her family's fortunes; she'd just been grateful things were slightly less strained at home.

'It was normal.' He lifted his shoulders, but there was something in his eyes that had her waiting for him to elaborate. After a moment, he did. 'I was born into money but my father lost almost all of it.' She leaned forward and beneath the table their knees brushed so she almost jumped out of her seat, jerking them away. His eyes showed a hint of speculation but he reached down and put his hand on her knee, holding them where they were then stroking her flesh so stars began to dance against her eyelids.

'How?' Her question was husky, coated by her unmistakable desire. 'I would have thought that to be impossible, given your wealth.'

'Bad investments. Messy divorces.' Santos grimaced.

'Plural?'

'Plural indeed. He's currently on wife number nine, and that marriage looks like it has just about run its course.'

'Nine?' she repeated, her eyes wide with disbelief. 'How in the world…?'

'He's a hopeless romantic.' Santos said the words lightly enough but she felt the undercurrent of irritation, his strong sense of disapproval. 'Each wife is younger than the last—my current stepmother is my junior by several years.' He shook his head.

'And the divorce settlements are expensive?'

'Were.' His lips were a grim line. 'He signs pre-nuptial agreements now, limiting what his wife is entitled to.'

Was it any wonder Santos had proclaimed a distaste for marriage and commitments?

'But the first few, when I was still a boy and a teenager, were costly. The fortune was divided, and divided again, so it was left to me at eighteen to take over the running of things. My grandfather had taught me from a young age and I enjoyed it—I lived and breathed the business and had a knack for investments. It took me the better part of a decade but I shored up our interests and transferred away from old corporate strategies to more nimble, digitally based options.'

'Impressive.' And she meant it. His business acumen must have been brilliant, given what his father had done to their wealth.

'Not really. It's just where my talents lie. Did you always want to be a teacher?'

The rapid-fire conversation change had her shaking her head before she could stop herself. 'No. I took a pretty circuitous route to this occupation, actually.' The wine was spicy and made her feel warm as she sipped it.

'Via mathematics at the Académie?'

'Right.' She chewed on her lip, wondering at the temptation to speak honestly with him when she made a habit of keeping her background to herself these days. Having been a child prodigy, trotted out for newspapers and television talk shows, had taught her how valuable discretion was. Additionally, most people tended to be intimidated by her, or became too embarrassed to speak honestly, as though she might be critiquing their sentence structure on repeat. Isolation had been part and parcel of her life as a child and teen. For the first time, it played no part in her life; she generally ensured it stayed that way by not mentioning her academic career.

'What were your other specialities?' It was as though he knew how close she was to opening up to him and understood exactly the question to ask.

'Physics.' She looked at her wine as she spoke. 'My first degree was in physics. My postgraduate as well.'

'First degree? How many do you have?'

'Three.'

His surprise was obvious even without looking at him. She felt it in the way he shifted in his chair and in the tone of his voice. 'Three?'

Heat flushed her skin. She ran her fingers along the stem of her wine glass.

'No wonder you never got around to having sex. When in the hell would you have found the time?'

He laughed and she found herself laughing with him, shaking her head a little, but a moment later he was quiet, leaning forward and putting his hand over hers. Sparks flew through her veins, startling her with their intensity.

'You've been teaching for a few years. It doesn't add up.'

'No, probably not,' she drawled, and then words began to drop from her mouth without her conscious decision. 'I graduated my physics degree at eleven. Maths at thirteen. I got my doctorate at fifteen then decided to study education.' She lifted her shoulders. 'I would have gone straight to teaching, but I was too young at sixteen, obviously, so spent a few years working with space agencies and doing some research projects.'

He was silent. When she lifted her eyes towards him he was staring at her as though she'd relayed all of this in an alien language.

'You're some kind of genius.'

'I don't really like the term genius,' she said after a slight hesitation. 'It's often misunderstood, certainly misapplied, and it's incredibly elitist. I have particular aptitudes. Where your strengths lie in business, mine are in mathematics and science. I was born being able to comprehend it and, because that's reasonably unusual, was given unbelievable opportunities to develop that predisposition.'

'Fine, not a genius,' he said with a shake of his head, his beautiful blue eyes roaming her face. 'How old were you when your parents realised you were—gifted?'

She sipped her wine, the myth of her brilliance one she'd heard her parents tell in interviews—interviews they'd been paid for, of course—so many times, she could almost repeat it verbatim. 'I spoke in full sentences at six months of age. That's unusual, but actually in people with extraordinarily high IQs it's common.' She flushed. 'I appreciate how that must sound—'

'It sounds like you have a nose on your face, two eyes in your head and an extraordinarily high IQ,' he interrupted quietly, squeezing her hand. His words, and the simple acceptance of her brain's abilities as merely something she'd been born with, filled something in her she hadn't realised had needed filling. She nodded, just a small, involuntary movement.

'By the time I turned one, I was reading and comprehending full books. At eighteen months, my parents had enrolled me in a monitoring programme that's a global initiative. Children like I was are watched, tested, bench-marked endlessly. Sometimes, though it's rare, a child can exhibit early signs of high IQ and then simply plateau. For those that don't, the programme tracks development and finds placements that will, theoretically, stimulate cognitive skills.'

'What kind of placements?'

'I undertook several subjects at Walsh when I was five.' Amelia named the American Ivy League that had been her first introduction to education. 'From there, I spent two years in Japan, at the Nagomyaki Institute, and so on and so forth.'

'Your family moved around a lot, then?'

'They came with me, at first, but after a year or two they returned to their normal lives and left me at school to study.'

Amelia's eyes met Santos's and saw something in their depths that pulled at the fibres of her being.

'You travelled on your own? To America?' His frown was harsh, his disapproval obvious.

What could she say? She felt the same way, now that she was an adult. 'America, Japan, Sweden. I was very capable,' she offered by way of excusing her parents, even when emotionally she couldn't really justify their actions. 'But it was hard,' she said on a sigh. 'I was still a child and I think there was an expectation that emotionally I was on par with my intellectual abilities. I wasn't. I used to get nightmares, terrible nightmares, and all I wanted was my mum.' She shook her head a little, the maudlin thoughts the last thing she wanted to consider. 'Anyway…' she tapered the word off, lifting her shoulders. 'That's ancient history.'

He took a drink of his wine, then placed his glass between them. 'Where do your parents live now?'

Something sharp jabbed her inside. 'They're in London.' She spoke carefully but the words were still rich with emotion.

'Do you see much of them?'

She swallowed past the lump in her throat. Six years and it was still almost impossible to accept the state of her relationship with her mother and father. 'We're estranged.'

'Because they sent you around the world when you were practically young enough to be in diapers?'

Her expression lifted a little into a tight smile. 'It's at their choosing, not mine.'

He was watching her with obvious surprise. 'Why?' he prompted eventually, when she didn't elaborate.

'Because I opted to become a teacher. And teaching isn't a particularly well-remunerated or regarded profession—at least, not like being a world-renowned astrophysicist.'

His features showed his lack of comprehension. 'And so?'

She took a small sip of the wine then pushed the glass away. As delicious as it was, the fact she didn't drink often meant it was already making her feel a little light-headed and tingly. Or maybe that was Santos's proximity and having the full force of his attention.

'And,' she continued slowly, to give the words less time to hurt. 'We were really poor. My dad was a welder, and didn't have a lot of work; Mum wasn't qualified for anything so took work when she could but, when I came along, they were paid all this money—'

'By whom?' he interrupted, business-like as he honed in on the facts of what she was saying.

'By the programme conducting research, initially— they were paid annually to keep me enrolled. There was a lot of media attention too and they had an agent who found them interviews and the like. Then, colleges were vying for me to attend, and in the end it came down, largely, to how much they were willing to pay. I didn't know any of this.' She shook her head, the words a little scathing even when she'd long ago made her peace with the financial aspects of it. That wasn't what really hurt.

'That's exploitative.'

'They were very poor, Santos.' She gently defended them.

'Perhaps; but, while I don't think that's necessarily any justification, I was referring to the universities.'

'Ah.' She nodded. 'I got a lot out of it, though. I hated leaving my parents, I hated being away from home, but

I loved the learning. I was challenged and pushed for the first time in my life.'

He nodded thoughtfully, easing back in his chair. Her hand was cold compared to the warmth of his touch moments ago. 'You were their meal ticket.'

She winced at the phrase, but it was accurate. 'Yes.'

'And they came to consider your income as theirs?'

Her face paled a little. 'They managed my income,' she said softly. 'When I began to consult at space agencies, any payment was being handled by dad. He took a management fee.'

'A considerable one?' Santos's voice was flattened of emotion, but not enough. She heard the disapproval there and ingrained protective instincts that had her lifting her shoulders. 'I'm not really sure.' It wasn't true. After they'd argued, she'd taken the reins of her own career and had realised how much money had been flowing through her bank account—both in and out. The reality of that had almost broken her.

'And so at five years of age you sat through courses designed for—what?—sixteen-year-olds?'

He brought the conversation back to her studies. She lifted her brows in silent agreement.

'You didn't have any friends your own age?'

She pulled a face. 'I didn't have any friends at all,' she said seriously. 'What teenager wants to spend time with a child?'

'But as you got older?'

'I was still young and, by then, pretty socially awkward. What I had in academic ability I absolutely lacked socially. But eventually, yes, I met someone—a friend. He was the first person to introduce me properly to the Classics, and through them I learned so much about emotion and motivation.'

'And you're still friends?'

'Yes. We're close.' She smiled. 'He's very important to me.'

She wondered at the slight shift in Santos's expression to something like speculation. 'And yet you and he never…?'

'Never…?' she prompted, even when she knew what he was asking.

'You weren't intimate?'

'No. Brent's like my only family now—there's no way I'd ever do anything to ruin that.'

'So you might have been interested in him but for the fact you don't want to confuse friendship with sex?'

She ignored the jangling of nerves in the pit of her stomach. 'Until I met you, I'd never known anyone I wanted to have sex with.'

His eyes swept shut for a moment, his expression impossible to read.

'Amelia…' There was a warning tone in his voice. She ignored it.

'I'm only being honest.'

'It shouldn't have happened.'

She made a noise of frustration. 'Yeah, well, it did. Are you going to ignore me for the rest of the time I'm here?'

He angled his face away. 'It's for the best.'

She stared at him, frustration eating her, but whatever doubts she'd had earlier his determination to box away what had happened, as though it was a simple aberration they could both forget, filled her with a sense of absolute determination.

'Are you seriously going to sit there and act as though you can just flick a switch and feel nothing for me?'

He turned to face her, his eyes showing impatience. 'I don't *feel* anything for you.'

'I'm not talking about emotions.' She rolled her eyes. 'I mean chemistry. Desire. Lust.'

He ground his teeth, his jaw tightening with the movement. 'What do you want from me?'

'I want you to look at me. I want you to stop ignoring me and pretending it didn't happen. I want you to acknowledge that you still want me.'

When he turned to face her, his expression was like granite. 'It shouldn't have happened.' He stood, scraping the chair back.

But she wasn't ready for him to simply walk away from her.

'You keep saying it shouldn't have happened, but I wanted it to! And I'd do it all again. I'd do it again right now, if you weren't acting like a coward, too scared to face up to this.'

He made a growling noise. 'You have no idea what you're talking about.'

'Don't I? Or is this what it's like for you? You have sex with a woman and then move on without a backwards glance?'

'Generally, yes.'

She blanched a little, so he felt a wave of remorse.

'But we are living in close quarters for the next few weeks and, believe me, ignoring you is best—for both of us.'

* * *

Amelia had waited up on purpose but the sight of Santos striding into his home still hit her with an unexpected wave of sensation. Emotions fired through her, and her body responded in kind, as though recognising its master. How she hated that.

'Amelia?' He stilled, his eyes sweeping over her in that way he had. 'What are you doing awake?'

'I want to talk to you.'

He compressed his lips. 'We've already spoken.'

'It's not about us.' Hurt lanced her, his easy dismissal making her feel like a nuisance. 'It's Cameron.'

Wariness crept across his features. He moved towards her, pausing a few feet away, a safe distance, but none the less her senses went into overdrive.

'Go on.'

'I get that you're ignoring me, but if the by-product of that is you ignoring him, not being home the whole time he's awake, then my being here is completely pointless.'

'I disagree. You being here is meant to help Cameron adjust to life on the island, life in Greece. You're doing that.'

'And what about helping him adjust to you?' she pushed, her eyes loaded with feeling.

'I told you, my relationship with my son is not your concern.'

'That's ridiculous,' she retorted angrily. 'How can you say that?'

'He's *my* son.'

'Not that you'd know it,' she retorted, then wished she hadn't when he took a step backward, as though physically reeling from her comment. She took in a breath, needing to remember how to stay calm when calm was the opposite of how she felt.

'Look, when I'm not here, you're going to need to know how to be some kind of father to him. You've uprooted him, dragged him across to Greece, and for what? So he can be pampered by people he doesn't know?'

'He has you.'

She shook her head. 'I'm not enough. You're his *father*. And if the reason you're staying away all day and into the night is because you don't want to see me then I'll go away again, Santos.'

'Don't threaten me.'

'I'm not threatening you. I will pack my bags and leave tomorrow unless you promise to start spending time with him.'

'It's not that easy!' His voice was raised and there was something in his features, a sense of panic or disbelief; she couldn't say. He controlled his temper, lowering his voice. 'It's not that easy.'

'It's not meant to be easy. He didn't choose to lose his mother, and you didn't choose to discover you're a father to a six-year-old boy, but that's the situation.' She held his gaze. 'If the idea of seeing me is so distasteful to you—like you're worried I'm going to throw myself at your feet or something—then don't. Believe me when I tell you, I'll very happily go to the other side of the island when you're in the house, if that's what it takes.' She glared at him to underscore how serious she was. 'Just spend time with your son, Santos. He needs to know you.'

CHAPTER NINE

KNOWING SHE WAS right did nothing to mute his irritation. In fact, it only served to increase it. What the hell had he been doing?

He'd brought Cameron to Agrios Nisi and sooner or later he had to find a way to draw him into his life. He had to break through the barriers and forge some kind of connection with his child.

Amelia was completely right. Worse, she was right that he'd let a need to control the desire he felt for her come between spending time with his son. That was unforgivable and yet it was also confirmation.

Confirmation that he was more like his father than he cared to admit. Completely incapable of giving his son what he needed.

But that didn't give him an excuse not to try.

'Cameron?' He found the boy building a spaceship out of plastic bricks in his room, and watched him for several moments before crouching down at his side.

'It's a Jedi cruiser.'

Santos's smile was instinctive. 'You like building star ships?'

'I guess so.' Cameron shrugged and Santos's heart went out to him.

'What else do you like?'

Cameron's eyes were exactly like his own. Santos stared into them as something beat across his heart.

'I don't know.' Another shrug.

'Do you like the beach?'

'I never saw the beach before I came here.'

Anger flashed in his belly; he ignored it. 'I have a yacht, you know.'

Cameron hesitated a moment. 'I like building yachts.'

'Do you?'

'Mmm… Big ones. All white. I make the sails out of paper. Sometimes fabric. Once I cut up a shirt of Mum's and she was very cross.'

The little boy's skin grew pale. He jerked his gaze back to the bricks, fumbling with them a little. His fingers weren't steady and he jabbed his space ship, knocking it so it fell to the floor and broke apart.

They both stared at it for several seconds.

'Let me help you,' Santos offered, wondering how long it had been since he'd played with bricks.

'No.' The word was firm, surprising Santos.

'You want to do it on your own?'

'I want you to go away.' He glared at Santos with a mutinous expression. 'I want to be alone.'

Something flared inside Santos. 'Cameron.' He spoke gently, not exactly sure how to handle the outburst. 'I know you'd worked hard on building that, and you're disappointed it's broken, but there's no need to speak like that. I was only offering to help. If you'd prefer to build it on your own, then I will just sit and watch. Is that okay?'

'I want you to go!' He pressed his palms into his eyes and then made a small sobbing noise, but he swallowed it, fixating on anger instead. 'Go away!'

Santos wasn't used to being told what to do but the boy was clearly distressed. He stood quickly, hovering for a moment, before walking towards the door. He was only two feet down the corridor when the door was unceremoniously slammed shut behind him. He winced, shaking his head, a rush of frustration exploding through him.

It wasn't Amelia's fault, but that frustration turned towards her, so he found himself walking through the house—at four o'clock on a Tuesday, when he should have still been in his office—in search of the woman who'd guilt-tripped him into doing something that evidently neither Santos nor Cameron wanted.

He found her by the pool, wearing a red one-piece bathing suit. He ignored his body's now predictable response. 'Santos?' She stared at him in obvious surprise, scrambling to her feet. 'What are you doing here?'

'What do you think?' He didn't mean to stand so close, close enough to smell her vanilla and strawberry body wash teasing his nostrils. 'I came home to spend time with my son.'

Her smile was like a ray of sunshine, piercing the fiercest storm cloud. But it didn't pierce his mood. 'I'm so glad, Santos.' She lifted a hand to his arm on autopilot, pressing it to his flesh. He fought an urge to pull away.

'Don't be. He threw me out of his room.'

She stared at him for a second and then laughed, the sweetest sound, something that threatened to unpick his anger. But he wouldn't let it. He *was* angry, and he was lost—completely lost. He'd never wanted to be a father!

'I'm sorry.' She sobered when she realised he was glowering at her. 'It's just the idea of anyone, let alone a sweet six-year-old kid, physically throwing you from anywhere is kind of absurd.'

'He told me to get out, in no uncertain terms.'

Amelia blinked at him, shaking her head. 'That doesn't sound like Cameron.' Her eyes narrowed. 'What did you say to him?'

'Nothing!' Santos growled. 'He was playing with bricks. I complimented him on the ship he'd built. I told him I have a yacht. I was about to suggest we go out on it for the afternoon and then he just lost it.' He expelled an angry breath. 'He broke his construction. I offered to help fix it. He snapped.'

'He's a little boy,' she said quietly. 'With big emotions. You just have to be—'

'Patient, yes, you've said that. Then let me be patient. Let me do this in my own time. You're the one who pressured me to spend time with him but he's not ready.'

'He's not or you're not?'

'Don't psychoanalyse me.'

'Well, then, don't be so childish,' she retorted. 'You know what? He might have thrown you out of his room but he'll calm down, and he'll see that you came to him, that you made the effort. It's not always going to be plain sailing but learning to trust that you'll be there for him is what you need to work on. Let him calm down now, then later go to him again. Let him see that even though he lost his temper you still love him. Trust me, he needs to see that.'

'What do you base this on?'

She spoke without thinking. 'Years of knowing what it feels like to have no one in your corner.' She wished she hadn't been so honest when his features showed obvious curiosity. 'Give him time. And keep doing this. Come home, spend time with him. Be in his life without pressuring him.' She dropped her hand to curve over his, entangling their fingers. 'Okay?'

His fingers gripped hers right back, his features taut, revealing nothing, so she had no way of knowing what he intended until his head had swooped down and his lips claimed hers, his tongue driving into her mouth, his body curving around hers, the kiss filled with passion, anger and annoyance. And she felt those things too, biting through her, so she kissed him back with the same intensity, grinding her hips, frustration exploding in her gut.

'I wanted to ignore you,' he growled, but his hand lifted to the back of her head, holding her there so his mouth could ravage hers, dominating her in every way.

'You have been.'

'Not well enough. Not really.' And then he was lifting her, pulling her towards the pool house, his body so strong and powerful, hers so full of need that it didn't even enter her head to demur, to put a stop to this.

They'd been fighting over Cameron, but was it possible they'd really been fighting each other, this instinct, looking for another way to satiate the violent needs somersaulting through them?

He kicked the door shut behind them, moving her to the bed, dropping her onto it but staying standing, looking down at her.

'*Thée mou, voítha me,*' he said intently. 'What am I doing?'

'You're making love to me,' she said simply. 'And it means nothing, except that in this moment I want you and you want me,' she promised, sitting up so she could reach the button on his jeans. 'You don't need to worry about hurting me.'

He chased her to the bed, though, stripping his clothes as he went before turning his attention to her bathers, pulling them from her body as quickly as he could, revealing her nakedness to his hungry gaze.

'This is madness.' He pushed the words into his mouth as his hands ran over her body, worshipping her curves.

'Yes.' She kissed him right back, hard and fast, wrapping her legs around his waist, drawing her towards him. He swore softly, breaking away from her just long enough to pull a condom from his wallet— he'd begun to carry them as a precaution after last time, which should have told him how realistic he found the whole 'ignoring her' approach.

'Amelia?' Sanity was almost gone but there was still a thread—just enough. 'Are you sure?'

She pushed at his chest in response, flipping him to his back. 'I've never been more sure of anything in my life. Make love to me. Now.'

* * *

'Christos.' He turned to face her, his eyes showing complete surprise. He wasn't sure he'd ever had such fast sex. What had it been—ten minutes? He felt as though a whirlwind had raced through the pool house. They'd rolled off the bed, onto the floor, knocking over a bedside table and lamp at some stage. Usually, he liked to savour the experience but passion—everything—had overwhelmed him completely.

'Don't freak out.'

It was such a ridiculous thing for Amelia to say—such a mirror of his own sentiments—that he laughed. 'I'm not, believe me.'

'Okay, good. It's just, last time, you totally freaked out.'

He propped up on one elbow, looking down at her. 'I did. A little. I hadn't expected it. Then or now.'

'No,' she agreed, staring up at the ceiling before shifting her gaze to his face. 'I like being with you.'

A warning light flared inside his brain.

Don't freak out.

'I know who you are,' she said quietly. 'And what your limitations are. I'm just saying I like being with you. I don't think you should go back to ignoring me again.'

Mortified, he angled her face towards his. 'I have no intention of it. That was to protect you, not to hurt you. I was trying to simplify everything. It didn't work and I was wrong.'

'Yes, you were.' She smiled, though, reaching up and running a hand through his hair. 'So what do you intend, then?'

His chest tightened.

Don't freak out.

'Because I'm only here for a bit under a month, and neither of us wants to get involved in anything serious. But I do want to do this again. And again. And again.'

He laughed. 'I get the picture.'

'So what if we agree that we just…keep it simple?'

'It's not simple, though, *agapitós*. Cameron adores you. If this ends badly…'

'It won't.'

He shook his head. 'You don't understand. I witnessed enough relationship breakdowns in my childhood. They're difficult to watch from the side-lines. Seeing people you care about hurt each other is not something I want for my son.'

'First of all, this isn't a relationship. Not in that sense. It's just an…arrangement.' She grinned, the sexiest smile he'd ever seen. 'And, besides, we can make sure no one knows about this.' She shrugged. 'Especially Cameron.'

'And can you say with confidence that you will feel that way in five weeks' time, when you leave the island?'

She laughed, shifting a little, bringing their bodies into more intimate contact. 'You think you're so irresistible, don't you?'

His eyes held a warning.

'You think every woman on earth is at risk of falling in love with you.'

'I didn't say that.'

'I'm more worried that *you'll* fall in love with *me*,' she said with an impish lift of her shoulders, drawing his gaze to the dusky pink aureole of her nipple. 'After all, I'm quite unique, you know.' She laughed, to show she was joking, but he didn't.

His expression was deadly serious. 'I don't believe in love—not romantic love, in any event. I don't ask you not to love me because I'm arrogant, so much as because it's utterly futile. I will never return it. This is just sex.'

A small smile moved across her face as she lifted her head, resting her chin lightly on his bare chest. He slept. Breath moved in and out, rhythmically, reliably; beneath her his heart beat, strong, regular, deep. Day was just preparing to break, whispering its promise beyond the window, urging the night to fade into nothingness, emerging in a blaze of triumphant orange somewhere near the horizon. It had been a warm night and they'd fallen asleep with the windows open. The curtains billowed a little, adding to the magic of that pre-dawn moment.

Do you think I want to wake up beside you every morning I'm here?

She'd thrown those words at him after they'd first slept together, the absurdity of the expectation making them ring with defiance in that moment.

But it was exactly what she'd done several times now in the three weeks since that afternoon in the pool house, when they'd both been so angry and passion, tension and need had spilled over, offering them the best kind of balm.

She woke early—it was part of her make-up, her overactive mind rousing her into the day well before light broke across the sky—and she never stayed in his room once she was awake. But this morning, she was tempted.

New to the ways of intimacy, she hadn't realised that hunger could be impossible to satiate. She couldn't have understood that each time they were together only seemed to increase her dependency on him, not lessen it as she'd anticipated.

Desire hammered through her veins now, thready and demanding, so that she ignored her usual pattern of behaviour—sneaking back to her room before anyone else was awake. Instead, she slowly eased the sheet from his broad, tanned body, exposing him inch by delicious inch, her eyes feasting on a chest that was broadly ridged—so familiar to her now that, despite her lack of artistic talent, she knew she could easily and confidently sculpt it from clay, just from memory alone. When the sheet reached his waist he moved just a little, shifting in his sleep. She stiffened, staying perfectly still, her eyes locked to his face until his breathing had resumed its steady, rhythmic pattern.

She pushed the sheet down his thighs lower still and then let it drop back to the bed with an almost silent swish, pressing against him. She bit down on her lip, her pulse rushing through her at an unbearable speed, and then she moved slowly in the bed, her eyes on his face as she moved.

He worked long hours. Despite the beauty of this island, he left it each morning at seven-thirty, like clockwork, and returned about twelve hours later. He spent around half an hour with Cameron then, and she

worked, trying not to think of him when the fact he was
in the house made it almost impossible to concentrate.

They only saw each other at night. And every night
had made her more aware of her body's needs and likes,
of what she was capable of, of what she could feel,
of how all-consuming physical desire was, until she
found herself wondering how she'd ever existed without something as biologically imperative as sex.

He had driven her wild, showing her how her body
liked to be pleasured, using his fingers, himself, his
mouth, to drive her to orgasm after orgasm.

With a small smile tingling her lips, she dropped her
mouth over his arousal, his guttural noise in response
shooting barbs of pleasure through her. She felt him
shift, and when she blinked her eyes towards his face
saw that he was watching her, his eyes still heavy with
sleep, his lips parted in slumberous sensuality.

She'd never done this before—never even imagined doing something so intimate, at first—but as he'd
continued to teach her what her body was capable of,
she'd begun to harbour fantasies of how she could visit
that upon him. She knew her experience might make
her less than spectacular, but feminine instincts were
driving her, so she moved her mouth up and down his
length, letting her tongue brush over his tip before
pushing him deep into her mouth once more, so he
hitched against her throat. She made a small murmur
of appreciation—he was so large, so hard; and, as she
continued to take him deep into her warmth, he spoke
in Greek, low and husky, the words impossible to comprehend, yet she grasped his meaning.

He was as filled with desire as she had been the

night before, when he'd lashed her with his tongue, his strong hands holding her legs apart, permitting him full access to her femininity.

'Amelia, please.' There was a plea in his words but she didn't answer it. She didn't know what he wanted and she wasn't sure she cared. This was perfection. Feeling him like this, inside her, and seeing the answering wavering of his control, was some kind of fantasy come to life.

'You must stop.' His hand pressed at her shoulder. She paused, lifting her gaze to his while her lips stayed pressed to his tip.

'Why must I?'

'Because if you don't…'

'Yes?' She took him deep into her mouth then and he cursed—in Greek, yet his tone made the meaning of his word abundantly clear.

'Amelia.'

She laughed softly, the sound carrying across the room towards the ocean.

'Santos,' she said his name sternly. Then grinned. 'Relax.'

'Not bloody likely.'

She laughed again but, a moment later, neither of them was laughing. She moved faster, completely captivated by the intimacy of this and the ancient, feminine rush of power that trilled in her veins. Driving him beyond wild was possibly the most addictive thing she'd ever done. His fingers dug into her shoulder, and his voice filled the room, but she didn't stop, not until he'd surrendered to her completely, his pleasure exploding through her, his hoarse groan wrapping around her.

Lifting on to her haunches, she then straddled him, smiling, settling herself on his waist and pressing her hands to his chest.

He captured one of her hands as it trailed towards his nipple, lifting it to his lips instead and pressing a kiss against the inside of her wrist. 'Have you tried contacting your parents?'

For a moment, pain lanced her chest. She met his eyes then looked away towards the dawn sky and the shifting ocean beneath it. 'I call them a few times a year. They don't answer, and never return my calls.'

Her pain was obvious; she could feel it spreading through her and she forced a smile to her face. He didn't return it. 'Don't look at me like that, please.'

'How am I looking at you?'

'Like you feel sorry for me. Like you're working out how to fix it.'

His frown was a flash in his face. 'It seems strange that your parents would choose not to have you in their lives. And stranger still that you would accept it.'

'What can I do? You can't force someone to love you, Santos. It's taken me a long time to accept it, but at the end of the day my value to them was always tied up in my academic success, and how that translated financially for them. I—as a person on my own—don't particularly matter.'

'If that's true, then they don't deserve to have you in their lives.'

She couldn't respond to that. She'd come to a similar conclusion years earlier but that didn't take the sting out of it. She tried another smile and squeezed his hand. 'It's fine.' She wasn't sure if she was saying that to herself or him.

He was quiet for a time, so that only the sound of the ocean rolling towards the island broke the silence. A moment later, she shifted her weight away from him. 'I should get back to my room.'

'Oh, no you don't.' He grabbed her arms and tumbled her to the bed, his body weight on top of hers now.

She laughed, pressing a palm to his chest. 'What are you doing?'

'You can't wake a man up like that without giving him the honour of repaying the favour.'

'I think I'm still well and truly in your debt,' she said, her lips twitching with amusement, her heart hammering with anticipation.

'But who's keeping score?'

She couldn't reply. Not when his mouth wrapped around one of her nipples and his fingers moved between her legs, pushing all thoughts from her mind completely.

'What are you doing tonight?'

He watched as she pulled her clothes on, each movement unknowingly graceful, her body lithe and beautiful.

'I'm going to double-check some equations before I email them off, and then Talia and I had talked about taking Cameron to look for shells.'

He nodded distractedly, the activity perfectly suitable for a day such as this. And he had a mountain of work. But, in the back of his mind, he was conscious of the days racing past. Nights were a sensual blur, nights in which he could indulge his cravings for this woman piece by piece until—momentarily—he was satisfied. But mornings broke faster than he'd have liked, and she was always gone, a phantom of her in the throbbing of his pulse and the hardness of his body. In two weeks, she'd leave the island for good, and he was mostly relieved by that, because already he could see how easily he could become addicted to her. Addicted to her body, he reminded himself forcefully, because that was what he found himself waking up craving.

Sex.

And sex was something he understood. But there was something different with Amelia, the way being with her made him feel. Perhaps it was simply her presence on his island, a haven he generally kept private. Or perhaps her fierce intelligence added another dimension to their dynamic—he certainly found them sparking off each other in a way that was wholly new. Or perhaps it was everything about her.

Whatever the reason for his fascination with her, he'd be glad when she left. It would be liberating not to feel this drugging sense of desire in every waking moment, and once she left the island she'd take with her temptation. He wouldn't think of her again—not often, anyway.

But for now, she was here, and he wasn't foolish enough to look a gift horse in the mouth. 'I have to go to the office this morning, but I thought I could come back earlier. Around lunchtime.'

She slowly turned to face him. 'Oh.'

It wasn't exactly the reaction he'd expected. That

dredged a grim smile to his face—since when had Amelia reacted as he'd expected?

'I'm not invited to collect shells?'

'Of course.' She shook her head. 'I could use a full day to work.'

He narrowed his eyes. 'I meant to come with you.'

'I don't think that's a good idea.' She tucked her shirt into her trousers, her narrow waist drawing his attention before he transferred it back to her eyes.

'Why not?'

'Because we agreed Cameron—no one—would find out about us.'

'And you think collecting shells will be some sort of public declaration of intimacy?'

A blush coloured her cheeks. He loved how easily she did that.

'No, of course not.' And then a second later, 'But there's an inherent risk to it. When you and I are together, and no one else is around, there is a zero per cent chance of someone learning about this. Those odds increase exponentially if we throw in an afternoon with Talia and Cameron.'

'Fine, then,' he said, wondering why her response was so frustrating to him. 'Then come to Athens with me today.' Her eyes were huge in her face, and she shook her head numbly.

'If I wouldn't agree to an afternoon here on your private island, why in the world would I agree to go to Athens?'

Exasperation made him expel a harsh sigh. 'Because it's beautiful and you'd love it?'

'I've been to Athens.'

Something like impatience burst through him. 'Not with me.'

'Besides.' She changed tack. 'Cameron is looking forward to looking for shells, and it would mean the world to him if you'd go with him. He's really warming to you.' She hesitated. 'You're making such progress.'

And he was. He'd followed her advice of a few weeks earlier, waiting for Cameron to calm down before approaching him again, keeping a safe distance, simply watching, letting him know he was there. He'd discovered a love for block building and, over time, he and Cameron had begun to work on a project together. As they worked, they talked, so that they were really getting to know one another. She didn't need to push him to spend time with Cameron any more; he did so because he enjoyed it.

'Let's make a deal.'

'I'm listening.'

'I'll spend the afternoon with Cameron.'

Her smile was like a burst of lightning, bright and fascinating, her nod one of obvious approval.

'And you'll have dinner with me.'

Her smile dropped and he tried not to think about how unusual that response was to a dinner invitation. 'Why?'

'Why not?'

'Because that's not… We agreed…'

'We agreed we wouldn't fall in love.' He laughed. 'Do you think you're so irresistible I can't sit across a table from you without formulating marriage plans?'

He intentionally turned her own words back on her,

reminding her of how she'd sneered at his arrogance early on in their relationship—or whatever this was.

'Fine, then. You've got yourself a deal. But don't you start getting all starry-eyed at my witty dinner repartee.'

He grinned, feeling a lightness move through him. 'I'll try my hardest.'

'This isn't exactly what I had in mind,' she drawled, staring out at the Acropolis. It was illuminated gently in the evening, golden lights washing over the ancient pillars.

'It's the best food in town.'

'And is it always empty on a Friday night?'

'You were worried about someone finding out about us.'

She shook her head. 'And so what? You booked out the restaurant?'

'Damen has known me a long time. He didn't mind.'

She shook her head, but she smiled—how could she not? 'Just as well I know how you feel about relationships because otherwise this could be construed as incredibly romantic.'

His skin paled so she had to bite back a laugh. 'It's not.'

She rolled her eyes. 'I'm joking.'

He relaxed visibly.

'How was shell hunting?'

His smile was natural and she felt something like relief spread through her. Cameron had been through so much. She wanted, more than anything, for him to connect with his father. It wasn't necessarily easy, given what he'd lost and the age he was at, but they were already making such inroads.

'He was quite excited by several of the "specimens", as he insisted on referring to them. I didn't want to tell him that shells such as these wash up along the shore all summer long.'

'He's a budding scientist,' she said proudly. 'He's got keen observation powers and an unquenchable thirst for knowledge.'

'And you are an excellent teacher to harness that.'

A man appeared, wearing dark trousers and white shirt. 'Here we are,' he said, a broad smile on his face. 'For the lady.' He placed a champagne flute in front of Amelia, and a beer for Santos, who nodded his thanks.

'Damen, this is Amelia Ashford, my son's teacher. Amelia, Damen has been running this restaurant since the dark ages.'

The older man laughed, rocking back on his heels. 'You make me feel old now, eh?' He reached out and, to Amelia's surprise, patted Santos on the head. He lifted a single brow but otherwise didn't respond.

'I've been coming here since I was an infant,' Santos explained when they were alone again.

Amelia couldn't hold back her grin. 'That's pretty sweet.'

'Sweet?' His laugh was gruff. 'I don't think I've been called that before.'

'I was calling Damen sweet,' she corrected with a saccharine tone. She sipped her champagne, then recalled what they'd been discussing before Damen had arrived.

'Where will Cameron go to school?'

Something tightened on Santos's face. A look of alertness. 'I'll meet with some headmasters next week.'

Her stomach rolled. 'Here in Athens?'

'Most likely.'

'So he'd travel over from the island? Or do you have a home nearby?'

He looked towards the window. 'I have a place not far from here. I prefer the island but the city will be more practical during term time.'

'I suppose this will mean a lot of changes to your life.'

He took a drink from his beer, holding her gaze over the rim. 'Yes.'

'So you're usually based on the island?'

'I consider it my home, but I spend a lot of time travelling.'

'Will you be able to curtail that now?'

'As much as possible.' He dipped his head forward. 'At least until he's settled into school and his new life.'

Her heart panged in her chest, his consideration not completely unexpected, yet it did surprise her. He obviously read that on her expression because his smile was almost self-mocking.

'You thought I would just carry on as I had before?'

'I hoped not,' she offered in response, running her fingers down the stem of her glass. 'He's a very special child and, after what he's been through, I'd love to think you could make him happy again.'

'Me too.'

'The thing is.' She shook her head, surprised by the admission she'd been about to make.

'The thing is?' he prompted when she didn't finish her sentence.

She sipped her drink and searched for the right

words. 'He can be quite anxious; nervous. I think that's one of the reasons I've always felt protective of him.' She tilted her head to the side thoughtfully. 'As a little boy, when he first came to Elesmore, he and I were in our first year together and I think we had the same first-day nerves.' Her smile was laced with nostalgia.

'Why did you decide to become a teacher?'

She sighed a little. 'Do you think it's strange?'

'Unusual,' he clarified, his grasp on the nuances of English flawless despite the fact it was a second language.

'I suppose it is. I could have done anything, and I did. I loved my work with the space agency, but it's teaching that I enjoy most.' She considered how to best explain that. 'I was given a lot of opportunities because of my IQ, but there's something valuable about helping everyone reach their potential, even kids who have to struggle to learn to read and get their heads around early maths.'

'And this is also why you chose a local comprehensive?'

'Instead of some kind of toffee-nosed public school? Is that the kind of place you went to?' she queried.

He tilted his head in silent confirmation. 'I went to the same school as my father, and his father and his father, went to.'

She smiled. 'Of course you did. Sometimes I forget you're part of some kind of dynasty.'

His smile quirked.

'I was drawn to a comprehensive, yes. I'm not so sure financial status should have any place in education.'

He sipped his beer, his eyes holding hers over the glass.

'Additionally, I felt that a public school would be more interested in promoting me to their parent body—the fact they had someone with my academic background on faculty would have become a selling point. Elesmore knew that anonymity was one of my requirements for accepting the job.'

'So none of the parents know about your previous life?'

'I prefer it that way. It's been my experience that, once people learn about that one fact of who I am, it becomes all they can see in me. I don't particularly like that.'

'You're more than your IQ?' He said it in a way that was teasing, so she smiled—an unusual response when she was discussing the pain and isolation that had resulted from her genius.

'It's just how my brain works.' She shrugged her slender shoulders and his eyes flicked lower, taking in the hint of cleavage exposed by the silk dress she was wearing. He reached across the table, lacing their fingers together in a simple gesture of intimacy.

'I like the way your brain works.'

She smiled, her eyes resting on their hands, hers a light gold and his a deep tan. 'Anyway, I met Cameron, and I've always felt an affinity with him. He's a very bright student, and quite sensitive. He feels things strongly, and that sometimes puts him out of step with his peers. Cynthia's death rocked him to the core.'

'Naturally.'

'I guess, I'm saying that I'm glad he has you—and

that you seem to realise the importance of being there for him right now.'

He squeezed her hand. 'I want to be a good father to him but it's not something I ever planned for. I was actually determined that I wouldn't have children.'

'Don't you need to continue the family name or whatever?'

'I have a half-brother for that.'

Surprise was evident on Amelia's face. 'You do?'

'Andreo, yes. He's married, and far more likely—or so I thought until recently—to be the one to provide the Anastakos heirs.'

'How does he feel about Cameron?'

'He's surprised, but looking forward to meeting him.'

'Does he work with you?'

'He runs our Asia Pacific operations.'

'You're close?'

'We're...products of the same upbringing.' He flashed a tight smile and she knew him well enough to know it foretold a subject change. She was getting close to something he didn't want to discuss.

'You had an unhappy childhood?' She squeezed his hand back, drawing his gaze there.

'You know about my childhood.'

'Your father's divorces.'

'Right.'

'And you were unhappy?' she pushed.

'I was ambivalent.'

She tilted her head to one side, analysing his explanation. 'In what way?'

His sigh was a fierce expulsion of air. 'Our home

life changed dramatically, year to year. Children cannot help forming attachments to the people they live with. I would come to care for my latest "stepmother" before my father would invariably end the marriage and I'd never see her again.'

Amelia's stomach rolled. 'You don't keep in touch with any of them?'

'Andreo's mother,' he said quietly. 'But not the others.'

'God, it sounds like some kind of club: the Ex Anastakos Wives.'

'With a costly entrance fee.' He shook his head.

'That's why you're so dead set against relationships?'

'Yes.' The directness of his answer surprised her. 'In my experience, nothing good comes from fooling yourself into believing you need another person to "complete" you, or whatever it is that makes people pledge their undying love.' His cynicism was obvious.

Damen appeared then, placing some delicious-looking meals before them—fried cheese, rice wrapped in vine leaves, lamb croquettes and some pitta bread with dips. The smell made Amelia's stomach growl—she hadn't realised how hungry she was.

'I saw these women almost broken by my father—their hurt and pain.' He shook his head in condemnation. 'I have no difficulty understanding his short attention span. I think in this way he and I are similar.' She ignored the sharp barb in her side. 'But he could simply have dated them and moved on when the interest faded. Marriage is so inherently filled with hope and promise—to offer himself to these women, only to bore of them within months.' Santos shook his head again, irritated. 'He is a living example of what I do not want to become.'

'And so you also view women as disposable, but you make sure they know that in advance,' she pointed out archly, only to encounter a heated look from him.

'Disposable is not the right word.' He frowned as he re-evaluated that. 'Or, if I were to describe a woman as disposable, I would expect her to say the same of me. I'm very careful on this score, Amelia. I don't enjoy the idea of hurting anyone.'

'You're *afraid* of hurting someone,' she corrected subtly. 'Your father has made you that way.'

His expression changed to one of shock. 'I don't think I'm afraid of anything.'

She laughed then, a soft sound. 'You're too tough for fear, right?'

He grinned in response, and the seriousness that his confession brought shifted, leaving an air of relaxed intimacy between them. 'Absolutely, *agapitós*.'

CHAPTER TEN

'DID YOU KNOW it took just a little over fifty years to build?' she asked, pointing up to the Acropolis. He resisted an impulse to tell her he knew pretty much everything about the world-famous landmark. Pride in his heritage had made him a scholar of the local history.

'And it is taking almost that long to repair it,' he joked, casually slinging an arm around her shoulders, drawing her closer to his body. It was a balmy summer's night and, though the sun had set, the air was still warm and humid. She was wearing a simple dress, but no less distracting for its simplicity. All night he'd been pulled between two desires—firstly to enjoy her company and conversation, and secondly to push at the flimsy spaghetti straps until the silk dropped low enough to reveal her neat, round breasts.

'I'd love to see what it looked like back then. The damage it's sustained is such a tragedy.'

'It's part of it, though,' he murmured in response, his eyes taking in the pocked pillars, the crumbling ruins that had been central to so many wars since its creation. 'Each mark tells a story and speaks to the building's defensive capabilities. It might look better without the damage but it would have a less rich history; it would have played a less vital part in Athenian society.'

'And that would make it less emblematic,' she agreed, looking up at him, her dark eyes intriguing and speculative.

'You said you've been to Athens. Was it to study?'

'I worked at the observatory for a few months.'

'You enjoy physics?'

'Yes, very much so.' She smiled again.

'You don't regret leaving it to become a teacher?'

'I didn't leave it. I made a conscious decision to continue my work, but I wanted to have another focus. I enjoy the challenge of physics, the possibilities and—it's strange to say it—the cathartic relief that comes from taking vast numerical sequences and wrangling them into some kind of order. It's a truly sublime process—up until a month ago, I would have said better than sex.' She winked at him and he laughed, pulling her closer, her body fitting perfectly against the ridges of his.

'And this wasn't enough for your parents?'

He felt her stiffen a little at his side.

'They didn't let me stick around long enough to explain that I wasn't abandoning my science work altogether.'

'Would it have made a difference?' A motorbike zipped past, loud and distracting. She waited until the sound had ebbed completely.

'I don't know. I think not—my desire for anonymity was at odds with their plans.'

'They enjoyed the fame that came with your success?'

She made a guttural noise of agreement.

'How come I haven't heard of you?'

'Well, outside of England I wasn't exactly famous,' she said with a self-deprecating laugh. 'It's not as though I'm the only person in the world with above-average intelligence.'

'What exactly is your IQ?'

Even in the moonlight he could see the heat that flushed her cheeks. Or perhaps he was simply familiar enough with her to know that she was modest—almost to a fault.

'You don't have to say if you would prefer not to.'

'It's fine.' She expelled an uneven breath. 'Around two hundred.'

He let out a low whistle. 'That's ridiculous.'

'It's just the way I was born.'

He stopped walking, wrapping his arms low around her waist and looking into her eyes. 'It's not a fault, Amelia.'

'I know that.'

'You shouldn't feel embarrassed by it.'

'I'm not. It's isn't the IQ that embarrasses me, it's people's reactions to it. It's being seen to exploit something that I had no hand in acquiring.'

'How is that different to what a supermodel does?'

She lifted her brows. 'You're calling me a brain equivalent to a supermodel?'

He laughed at that. 'Apparently.'

'I suppose everyone has different dispositions. Perhaps if my parents hadn't…'

'Gloried in your brilliance?' He was teasing her but

she was frowning, a little divot between her brows that he wanted to wipe away.

'They turned me into someone people knew about. They did interviews and got me in the papers; that was all part of it. For a while, my life felt like a circus. I had no control over where I went and what I did, and while I enjoyed the academic side of my life—I truly love studying and felt most at home when I was absorbing new information—I craved a normal childhood too. Friends, games, fun. Laughter. I don't think I laughed my entire childhood.'

He lifted a hand, cupping her cheeks, looking down into her eyes with genuine sympathy. 'You must have felt disappointed in them.'

'I do. But they're still my parents. I would have forgiven them—I can understand how difficult it would have been to bypass the opportunity to improve our financial standing—but they've cut me out of their life, Santos. I'm *persona non grata* to them and they did it so damned easily.' Tears sparkled on her eyes and something inside him shifted painfully.

'They were so angry with me. At first, I presumed they'd get over it. But they never did. They stopped returning my calls, changed their numbers, blocked my emails. I tried going to their home to speak to them— they moved house. I have no idea where they are now. I presume in London, because leaving it wouldn't make sense, but I don't know for sure. I bucked their plans and they cut me out of their life as though I meant nothing to them. To my mum and dad, my only point of merit was my intelligence—and what that meant for them. The realisation was one of the hardest I've ever come to.'

Santos was not a violent man. Having a front row seat to his father's life had taught him that all strong emotions had the potential to be disastrous, so he was generally guarded, but in that moment he wanted, more than anything, to shake her parents for what they'd done to her. Not only in shutting her out of their life but in turning her into their prize performer and neglecting to care for her whole self.

'You deserve better than that.'

Her smile was lopsided, a ghost on her face, haunted by grief. 'I felt worthless.' She lifted her shoulders. 'It was hard.'

She spun out of his arms and began to walk once more, her eyes trained on the Acropolis with its golden lighting. 'My friend Brent introduced me to the Classics a long time ago. I loved them for their dynamically drawn emotional peaks and troughs, but it was only once I was living my own Aristotelian tragedy that I could see what they were really about.'

Santos waited for her to continue.

'The purpose of a Greek tragedy is almost to purge you of grief, so, while you may watch the play and feel everything on the spectrum of sadness, there is an inevitable catharsis that comes after that—a relief from the pain that is supposed to result in an emotional lightness.'

He considered that, and in the back of his mind he wondered at her perspective on things, and how much he enjoyed her ability to weigh in on any subject. What did he expect? Intellectually she clearly blew him out of the water, but far from being threatened by that he wanted to absorb what he could from her.

'Did you feel lighter once you'd gone through the tragedy of your argument with them?'

'Eventually.' She said the word with a smile that was more like herself, light and simple, happy. Relief spread through him. 'It took a long time to accept the finality of what they'd done, and also how earnest they were in wanting me out of their lives. It wasn't so much their decision as the way their decision showed me that even my own parents thought of me as unimportant. Unlovable.' She winced a little, and her honesty had him wanting to rush to fill the silence with assurances. But what could he offer?

'None of this was your fault,' he said with firm determination. 'I don't know them but the impression I have is that your parents are absolute fools to have let such a trivial matter come between you.'

'The thing is, it wasn't trivial. Not to me. My vocation is a reflection of who I really am, in here.' She pressed her fingers between her breasts. 'I think teaching is one of the most worthy and important professions. In a thousand lifetimes I would always have chosen to be doing this. I love working with children; I love their optimism and potential and the fact they're little sponges, brains ready to learn and acquire information.'

Her passion throbbed inside his veins, her words carrying a physical weight that ran through him. It would be unfair to compare Amelia to the women he'd dated in the past—she was different from anyone he'd ever known, male or female—but he couldn't help thinking that she was the most captivating woman he'd ever slept with.

'If you became a bit of a minor celebrity in England, how have you been able to avoid recognition now?'

'I'm using my mother's maiden name,' she said simply. 'Grandma Ashford and I were close. When I chose to reinvent myself, it felt appropriate to honour her in that way.'

'So you're not completely alone?'

The light shifted from her eyes. 'She died a few years ago.' Amelia swallowed, her throat shifting. The moon cut through a cloud, bathing the footpath in front of them in silver light.

Amelia reached out a hand, as though she could touch it, then pulled it back almost awkwardly, her eyes jerking up to his.

'What is your actual name?'

She hesitated for only a brief second. 'I was born Amelia Jamieson.'

He hadn't heard of her, but that didn't mean anything. As she said, press coverage had probably been at its strongest in the UK.

'Well, Miss Ashford, I think you are brave and I think you deserve to be happy. I also think your pupils are incredibly lucky to have you.'

'I suppose we should go back to the island soon?' She glanced at her wrist watch, surprised to see it was almost midnight.

They'd walked all over Athens after dinner, with no destination in mind, simply a desire to be together, side by side. At least, she thought they'd had no destination in mind, but here, in an upscale neighbourhood surrounded by modern homes that were four storeys high, he nodded towards one.

'Or we could stay here?'

She wrinkled her nose. 'I'm gathering it's your Athens home and not just some stranger's place you think looks okay for a night's accommodation?'

He grinned and her heart skipped a beat. It had been a pretty perfect night. She felt so comfortable with him, but that didn't change the fact that every now and again he smiled, or looked at her with eyes that were smouldering, and she lost the ability to breathe altogether for how completely, heart-stoppingly handsome he was.

'It's my place.'

She eyed it, hesitating a little.

'It would probably be better for us to go back to the island.'

'Why?'

'Because if we spend the night here there's no way Talia won't put two and two together.'

'And get four. So?'

'I thought we agreed no one would find about this.'

'It's Cameron we care about protecting. Does it matter if Talia works out that we're sleeping together?'

Her heart skipped another beat, this one less pleasurably.

Does it matter if Talia works out that we're sleeping together?

Why did she want to pull at that sentence, to inject something else into it? Because they weren't just sleeping together. She'd felt more connected to him tonight than ever before and that wasn't about sex.

'It's your decision,' he said quietly, his eyes wandering across her face, studying her thoughtfully.

'It would be good to see where Cameron's going to live,' she conceded, after a beat had passed.

His smile dug right inside her. 'Come on.' His hand reached for hers and she put hers in it, smiling for no reason she could think of as they crossed the street together and took the stairs to his front door.

He didn't use a key. There was an electric pad and he swiped his watch across it, so it opened with a soft click. A light automatically came on and Santos stood back, gesturing for Amelia to precede him into the house.

A high-ceilinged corridor gave way to a staircase to the left and a lounge area on the right.

'Would you like a drink?'

'Perhaps a tea?'

He flashed her a grin at that but lifted his shoulders, detouring away from the living space to bring the kettle to life. She watched as he made their drinks—coffee for him, tea for her.

'Won't you be awake all night?'

His grin was laced with seduction. 'I can only hope.'

Her pulse slammed through her like a tidal wave; heat began to build low in her abdomen.

He led her upstairs then, and up again and again, until the steps narrowed, there were fewer and a small door opened onto the roof of the building, giving an uncompromised view of Athens and the Acropolis.

Above them, the stars shone against an inky black sky. She expelled a sigh of contentment, cupping her tea in her hands, watching as Santos pulled a brightly coloured blanket from a basket, spreading it across the roof, over the surface, before returning to the basket to retrieve some cushions. He scattered them over the blanket, then gestured for her to take a seat.

'Nice touch,' she drawled, using humour to defuse the fact that her heart was fluttering wildly inside her. She moved to the blanket, settling herself cross-legged on one side of it. He stretched out on his side, an arm propped beneath him, his body turned towards her. 'Is this a standard seduction routine, then? I imagine it works pretty well.'

She was sure she felt him bristle at that. 'Actually, I don't come up here often. I thought you would like the view.' He lifted his eyes towards the stars so she immediately felt childish for having waved his play-boy reputation between them. She winced and turned her attention to the ancient city sprawled before them.

'I do. Thank you.'

'Does it bother you?'

'What?'

'That I date a lot of women.'

'You mean sleep with a lot of women?'

He sipped his coffee and she could feel his eyes heavy on her profile. He didn't answer her question.

'Why would it?' She angled her face to his, her ex-pression carefully blanked of any emotional response.

'I'm so different to you.'

'Actually, you're similar to me in more ways than you're not.' She took a drink of her tea then placed the cup on the ground beside the mat, wriggling down to lie beside him, her body inverse to his, a mirror image of his position. On autopilot his hand curved over her

hip and her gut kicked with the anticipation that contact evoked.

'How so?'

'We're both loners, choosing to stay isolated from
any depth of human connection rather than be hurt by
someone we love. You do that by having meaningless
sex with whatever woman takes your fancy. I do it by
losing myself in my work and refusing to get involved
with anyone.'

She hadn't consciously appreciated it before that
moment, but as she spoke the words she realised how
true they were.

'In my case, it's more that I don't see the value in
that kind of relationship. I appreciate finding your "soul
mate"—' he said the word with derision '—and living
"happily ever after" might be the aspiration for many
people, perhaps even the meaning of life, but for me,
it's not. Everything I have seen has led me to believe
it's a flawed goal, and that people make themselves
unhappy by aspiring to it. I am not a loner. I enjoy the
company of others.'

'But on your terms,' she interjected softly.

He appeared to think about that a moment, then
nodded unapologetically. 'On terms that are mutually
agreed and which leave no room for misunderstand-
ing or hurt feelings.'

'I wonder if that's possible.'

'Why wouldn't it be?'

'Well, I don't know if emotions can necessarily be
so neatly corralled into order.'

'Which is why I keep them *out* of my life.'

Her smile was indulgent. '*You* do, but I'm not so

sure every single woman you've ever been with could say the same.'

'It's something I make clear before I get involved with a woman.'

She rolled her eyes, laughing a little. 'That's just a way of absolving yourself of guilt. People change. Someone might think one thing and then circumstances conspire to alter their expectations. You don't think it's possible that even one of the women you've been with wanted more from you than you were able to give?'

'If I thought that, I would end it immediately.'

'To save her from being hurt?'

'Exactly.'

'You've got it all worked out.'

'You're mocking me.'

'A little,' she conceded, reaching behind her for her tea and lifting it to her lips, then placing it on the mat between them.

'I think you're wrong.'

'Statistically, that's not likely.'

A grin flashed across his features. 'If you bring statistics into it then you have an unreasonable advantage in this argument.'

'I didn't mean for us to argue.'

'You're challenging my lifestyle.'

'I'm pointing out that it might not be as perfectly neat as you imagine, that's all.'

'And all the evidence tells me it is.' He lifted his broad shoulders and the hand on her hip began to shift, his fingers moving rhythmically over her flesh there, so holding onto her thoughts became difficult.

'Now you're pushing your own advantage.'

'Am I?' he challenged with mock innocence. 'How?'

'By making it impossible to think clearly.'

His grin showed he knew exactly what he was doing. Unapologetically, he dropped his hand to the bottom of her dress, sliding it up her thighs.

'I'm more interested in your dating life than mine, in any event.'

'What dating life?' she said with a small laugh. 'And why?'

'Because what I do is not uncommon. What you do is—'

'I know.' She flinched a little, the fact she had been a virgin until recently something that confused even her.

'You're a beautiful, fascinating woman. I find it impossible to believe you hadn't been asked on dates...'

At that, her feminism bucked hard. 'My not having really gone on dates bears no correlation to whether or not I was asked.'

He laughed softly. 'Naturally. So you just turned down any offers?'

'I accepted some,' she conceded. 'At Brent's urging. Good practice, he'd said, and I guess he'd been sort of right. But, honestly, I was so bored out of my brain I contemplated stabbing myself in the eye with a fork,' she joked.

He lifted his brows. 'So my witty and insightful conversation is how I won you over?'

'Nope, it's all down to sex appeal with you, sorry.'

'I'm flattered.'

'You probably shouldn't be. I'm basically reducing you to an object.'

'I don't think I mind.'

She grinned. 'I'm glad to hear it, because I intend to objectify you a lot for the next little while.'

'Why not start now?'

He thought she was asleep. She'd been quiet a long time, her head pressed to his chest, her hair loose along his arm. He'd been lying there, staring up at the stars overhead, replaying their evening: her rapid-fire conversation, a smile playing about his lips as he recalled the perfection of how it had finished—making love here beneath the ancient night sky.

'I always loved stars.' Her voice was a murmur.

He stroked her back, wondering what time it was. Two? Three?

He heard her yawn then she nuzzled in closer, her body cleaved to his. 'When I was nine, and incredibly homesick, I used to look out at the stars and imagine my mum. Did you know we're all made of stardust?'

'I thought that was just a song.'

'No, it's true.' Another yawn. 'Stars that go supernova create all the elements. We're more than ninety per cent stardust.' Her breathing slowed, and once more he thought she'd fallen asleep. Indeed, when she spoke next, her words were heavy, almost slurred.

'I used to look out at the stars and take comfort from the fact that, through them, my elemental make-up and my mum's, we were connected even though we were far apart. Stars bind us all together, in a way.'

CHAPTER ELEVEN

THE INTERNET WAS littered with articles about her, and photographs too. As Amelia Ashford had said, Amelia Jamieson had been in every broadsheet newspaper several times. But Amelia had also been modest. She'd told him some of her story without revealing many of the things others might have bragged about. Such as the scientific breakthrough she'd made as a ten-year-old that had led to a whole wing of a university in Texas being named after her. Or the research she'd done that had added a new dimension to the way scientists viewed star formation. She hadn't told him about the awards, the accolades, the grant money.

Her life, up until she'd made the decision to branch off from her scientific work and become a teacher named Amelia Ashford, had been completely different.

While he was in awe of her genius, he was even more in awe of her courage. To disregard the accolades and praise that was part and parcel of her success, to disappoint her parents and start a whole new life completely on her own, took guts and bravery. While he'd known she was special, seeing the full picture made him appreciate the full extent of that. Photographs of a young Amelia did something to his heart, layering cracks into it. She looked so young and so intensely vulnerable.

It also made a whole heap of sense when it came to why she'd turned up on his doorstep at Renway Hall like a lioness preparing to defend Cameron. She hadn't had anyone to stand up for her interests as a child, and she hadn't been prepared to let that same thing happen to Cameron.

It was hard not to feel a sense of affection for someone who was prepared to go in to bat for your own flesh and blood—and who'd single-handedly salvaged the relationship. Without Amelia, he didn't want to think about where he and Cameron would be.

'Working?' He propped one shoulder against the door of her office, scanning the whiteboards. Each was covered with incomprehensible mathematics. The first time he'd come in here and seen it he'd felt as though he were landing in a parallel universe. He was by no means intellectually lacking but his skill set was totally different from this. Mathematics was useful to him when it came to bonds, and profit and loss schedules, not these kinds of complex equation.

'Mmm…' She was scanning a piece of paper on her desk. She lifted her eyes to him, then a finger. 'Hang on one second.' Without turning away from him, she spoke again. 'Bishop to E7.'

Santos scanned the desk and saw that there was a tablet propped to her left. A man's face filled the screen. Handsome with blond hair, overly white teeth, a swarthy tan and green eyes. 'You're sure?'

She rolled her eyes but there was a wink in them for Santos. 'Absolutely. I have to go. I'll talk to you tomorrow?'

'No worries. Later, Millie.'

Millie? Heat shifted inside Santos. It wasn't jealousy so much as surprise, he told himself. He wasn't sure what he'd expected her friend Brent to be like—surely that was who she was talking to—but it hadn't been this.

'Playing chess?' He covered his unexpected response conversationally.

'I'm three moves away from check mate. He doesn't realise it.'

'You don't have a board.'

'It's in here.' She tapped her head.

He laughed. 'Of course it is.'

'Did you need something?'

Another burst of flame exploded inside him. It was the middle of the work day; it was unusual for him to be here, in her office. But the sense that he was unwelcome sat ill around his shoulders.

'You're busy?'

'I'm—no. Not really. Just familiarising myself with the class list for this year, starting to plan some lessons.'

This year. Term began soon; she'd be leaving. And, while it was strange to imagine what life on the island would be like without Amelia, he was also glad that their time together was almost drawing to a close. He wasn't foolish enough to pretend their forced proximity hadn't threatened to complicate his usually straightforward approach to relationships.

When Amelia left, he and Cameron would move to

Athens and he'd return to a normal sort of life. He'd meet other women, and before long he'd forget about Amelia.

No. He'd never forget about her, and he didn't actually want to, anyway. But, once she left, his life would return to normal; he wouldn't crave her like this. It was simply a question of proximity and habit.

'I'm going to stretch my legs on the beach. Want to join me?'

She blinked, the offer apparently not what she'd expected. 'Where's Cameron?'

'He's napping.'

Amelia's brows shot upwards. 'Napping? Is he ill?'

'He's exhausted,' Santos admitted sheepishly. 'I took him to the fishing village this morning. We hiked, swam, ate. I gather I wore him out.'

Her heart felt as though it were being gently warmed. Santos spending time with Cameron made her feel an intense wave of relief. When she'd first arrived she'd had no idea how Santos would ever fill the father role in Cameron's life but the pieces were falling into place. 'I've been meaning to ask about that—how come there's a village on an otherwise private island?'

'Come for a walk with me and I'll answer.'

She tilted her head a little. 'Bribery?'

'Absolutely.'

'Fine.' She dropped her pen and stood. The sight of her in a pair of linen shorts and a simple T-shirt made him want to forget his suggestion of the beach and instead drag her to his bedroom. He swallowed hard and spun away before he could do just that.

The sand was warm beneath their feet. He took her

hand on autopilot as they approached the shoreline, and felt her eyes jerk to his in response, but she looked away again almost immediately.

'So the fishing village?'

'Right. That was my grandfather.'

'He built it?'

'No.' Affection ran through him. 'My grandfather was a great man, Amelia. I wish…'

I wish you could have known him.

He cut himself off from saying the overly sentimental line, wondering where the hell the words had even come from. 'I wish he was still here, but he died when I was in my teens.' He kicked at the water; it splashed ahead of them. 'He was close friends with Daniel Konopolous, who was apparently renowned for his skill as a fisherman. In stormy weather and at any time of the day he could return with full nets. He lived on this island, but the village was losing its numbers, with people moving to the mainland. My grandfather bought the island, including the village, and allowed the fisherman to live and fish rent-free. There's been a fishing community here for a very long time; he didn't want to see that heritage lost.'

'And you still support the village?'

'I like having it here.' He reached down, picking up a piece of pale blue sea glass and handing it to her. She studied it as though it might have secret properties.

'So you don't charge them anything?'

'Why would I? I don't need the money.'

'I thought you lived and breathed business. Such generosity isn't routed in commercial principles.'

'Perhaps not,' he agreed. 'But it's born of decency.

Besides, I have no doubt my grandfather would come back and haunt me for ever if I made the slightest attempt to alter the arrangement.'

She was still looking at the sea glass. After a moment, she lifted it towards his face. 'This is the exact shade of blue as your eyes.'

The observation was simple, and perhaps it came from a scientific perspective, but that did nothing to stop the sharp blade that seemed to be drawing along his sides. And if he'd been wondering if she was reading something into that, or being sentimental in her own way, she lifted her hand and tossed the sea glass out to sea, smiling at him in a way that showed how wrong he was. What had he been afraid of—that she'd treasure the gift of sand-softened glass for ever?

She had done nothing to worry him on that score. Everything was going just as he would have wanted— simple, easy, no emotional demands. It was perfect. As if to cement that, he caught her around her waist and lifted her to his chest, so she tipped her head back on a laugh as he carried her out to sea.

'I'm fully dressed!' she warned and he arched a single brow in response.

'Is that an invitation?'

'Cameron could see.'

'He's fast asleep.'

She searched for something else to say but he didn't give her much opportunity. Striding deeper into the water, once it was halfway up his chest he dropped her into it and she squawked, spinning round and instinctively splashing him. He laughed, dropping into the sea himself, reaching for her, bringing her thrashing body closer and kissing her through the saltiness of the ocean.

She stopped moving and stood still, pressed to him, her body wet, their clothes clinging to them. When they kissed, nothing else seemed to have light or meaning; the world ceased to have a purpose beyond them. He deepened the kiss, his tongue duelling with hers, and she retaliated, using his body to move higher, her mouth pressing to his, her hands driving through his hair, her breasts flat to his chest. He groaned, moving deeper in the water until she was floating and he was keeping them standing, and only here in the safety of that depth did he push her shorts down, so he could cup her naked buttocks and hold her against his hardness.

The sun baked down on them, hot and unrelenting on the back of his head as he kissed her, his erection jerking between them, his body alive with a desperate hunger that only she could meet.

How could it still be like this between them? For weeks he'd been waiting for desire to wane, yet it hadn't. Every night together brought them closer to the end, making him aware of the temporary nature of this. And that served to increase his urgency, to make him yearn for her even at times like this—when they'd been together only the night before.

'You are so perfect.' He spoke the words in Greek, safe in the knowledge she wasn't fluent in the language and wouldn't understand them. 'This is perfect.'

Her response was a soft moan into his mouth and a roll of her hips, a silent invitation that came from her own overwhelming need for him.

'Please…' The word was one she said often when

they were making love, begging for him to quench her needs, and he never needed to be asked twice. He had no protection—a foolish oversight, but they had only been coming for a beach walk—he hadn't expected this. Why? Why hadn't he, when their needs were always paramount? And what had he wanted, then—simply to walk hand in hand and talk? Who the hell was he turning into?

In rejection of that, he moved his hand between her legs, his eyes on hers as he found her most sensitive cluster of nerves and strummed it, his fingers knowing exactly what she liked, how to pleasure her, how to drive her wild and then hold back, to extend her fevered need.

'I want you,' she insisted, tilting her head back, her eyes scrunched closed.

'I don't have a condom.'

'I do.' Her cheeks were already pink from the heat of passion but he suspected there was a blush in there too. 'It seemed like a wise precaution to start carrying something,' she explained with a shrug, reaching behind her and pulling a foil square from her back pocket.

'You have no idea how good that looks to me right now.'

'To both of us,' she assured him, using her teeth to open the square. Her hands found the tip of his cock and expertly rolled the protection over his length, if somewhat teasingly, so a hiss burst from between his teeth.

'Christos.'

Her response was to lift up and wrap her legs around his waist, taking him deep inside her, an inaudible curse escaping her lips as she lay back in the ocean.

His hands gripped her hips and he moved her, pulling her back and forth at first before his hand shifted to her femininity, strumming it as he moved so she whimpered and pulled to sitting, pressing herself against him and moving up and down his length, using her feet wrapped around his back for purchase.

Her first orgasm almost brought his own from him. He ground his teeth together, refusing to succumb to that temptation, needing more of this before he brought an end to it. Her breathing was frantic and he kissed her, sucking her panic and pleasure into his mouth, holding her against his body as her feminine core spasmed around his length.

Before she could find her equilibrium, he began to move again, pushing into her and pulling out, his hands roaming her body, his mouth devouring hers; or was it the other way around? A fever had gripped them both, making it impossible to tell who was pushing and who was taking; they were a jumble of hands and limbs and frenzied movements.

'God, Santos!' His name was tormented. She cried it out but the ancient ocean swallowed it away, the elements surrounding them making this all the more powerful. When her body was at its breaking point once more, he went with her, releasing himself with a guttural oath, burying his head in her shoulder, breathing her in, feeling every breath of hers in his lungs, his own lungs barely able to inflate his chest sufficiently.

The waves rolled with an audible gush; the ocean breathed alongside them and the sun beat down, the elements fierce and organic, and Santos stood there pressed to Amelia, holding her against his body until the world had tipped neatly back onto its axis.

'Your shorts are floating away.'

He lifted his head from her neck, confused at first before her words made any kind of sense. He angled his head to their left where, sure enough, his clothing was floating on top of the water.

'Mine too, come to think of it.' She laughed a little unsteadily.

'Stay here.' He pulled away from her with genuine regret, free-style swimming to their clothes and catching them in his palm.

'Thanks.' She took them from his outstretched hand when he returned. He put out an arm of support and she gripped it while she pulled on her shorts, smiling at him as though she was waking up from some kind of dream.

'That's not what I expected when we came out here.'

'Me neither, though I suppose that shows we should always expect it as a possibility.'

'That's true. One week a rooftop in Athens, the next a private beach in the Aegean.' She shook her head, her mouth curved in amusement.

'Tonight, a roof-top garden in Paris?'

'What?'

Her smile dropped, showing surprise. His tone was nonchalant, casual. 'I offered to take Cameron there, to measure the Eiffel Tower. I'm sure he'd enjoy it a lot more if you were there too.'

'Oh.' Uncertainty shifted in her expression. 'Are you sure?'

'Why wouldn't I be?'

'It's just… Paris.'

He waited.

'You know, city of love?'

He burst out laughing. 'And you think this holds some danger for us?'

Heat stole into her cheeks. 'No, that's silly.' She laughed, but it was shaky. 'But I'll have to get back to England soon. Paris might be better kept until after I go.'

'Paris is next door to London. Why not stop in on your way home?'

The finality of his offer filled her head with doubts. It was so casual, so carefree, as though 'the way home' was simple. As though a little detour would mean nothing. And it shouldn't. It wasn't the fact it was Paris, *per se*, but that it was yet another shared experience, something they were doing together. The night they'd spent in Athens had already begun to transform her dreams. Falling asleep in his arms beneath a starlit sky had seemed to weave her past and present together— fears and grief from her childhood, encapsulated by the heavenly spectre of glistening particles in the sky, had acted as some kind of balm. And ever since then she'd found it impossible not to think about that—and about him.

Santos had been clear about his wishes for this from the start, and she wasn't stupid enough to hope for more from him, but nor could she deny that she was starting to *want* more. The idea of returning to England was no longer one she faced with any degree of pleasure. Nor was her teaching job—though that seemed impossible to believe. Her village and school community were the first home she'd ever known but they weren't the only place she felt at home. Now, there was this island and this mansion, and even his place in Athens. It was anywhere Santos was.

A foreshadowing of disaster curdled her blood so that, as the Anastakos jet came down to land over the city, even the sight of beautiful Paris didn't arrest the worry inside her. Perhaps the real Greek tragedy of her life was still ahead of her.

'It's not getting bigger.'

Amelia met Santos's eyes over Cameron's head and smiled. It was a smile that hurt a little—everything hurt at that point. She knew she had to leave but that didn't stop her from feeling every single emotion.

'Not recognisably, no,' she answered, her voice a little raspy. 'It's a very gradual process that takes days of intense heat.' She tousled her fingers through his hair then reached down for his hand. His small one fit inside hers and she squeezed it.

'It's still beautiful.'

She smiled at Cameron again. 'Yes.'

'Mummy used to talk about the Eiffel Tower,' he confided as they began to walk along the Seine. Santos held Cameron's other hand in his and the three of them walked in a line.

'What did she say?' It was Santos who asked the question, his voice gruff.

'That it was one of the most beautiful things she'd ever seen.' His smile was tinged with sadness. 'She told me there's a very fast train that travels here and that we would take it one day.'

Sadness flooded Amelia. She glanced at Santos. His expression was steely. 'I'm sorry she isn't here to see it with us.'

She knew him well enough to know that he genuinely meant that. Her heart trembled a little.

'Me too.'

They walked in silence for a few hundred metres. 'Can I get some ice-cream?'

'No, darling,' Amelia murmured.

At the same time Santos said, 'I don't see why not.'

Cameron looked from one to the other and then leaned closer to Santos. 'Thanks, Dad.'

Santos couldn't help his reaction; his eyes flew to his son's face first and then to Amelia's. Her eyes sparked with his. They'd both heard it; they understood it. Dad.

Such a small word but the meaning... It ricocheted around them, exploding like a pinball inside Santos. Emotions he hadn't known he possessed welled inside him.

Dad.

He was a dad.

He closed his eyes for a moment, and when he opened them Amelia was smiling gently, her gaze warm on Cameron's little face. 'I'm out-voted, then.'

'Definitely.' Cameron licked his lips. 'Can I get two scoops?'

Santos laughed, a laugh that was so full of joy and pride; he was almost euphoric. Something about that moment felt utterly perfect. 'Don't push it.'

Santos's penthouse wasn't far away and, after picking up their ice-cream, they walked towards it, surrounded by the ambient noise of Paris. As they turned into his street, they were confronted by a night market. In the time they'd been out, it had been completely set up from scratch. Tents were side by side, lights had been strung from one side of a narrow walkway to the other and the stalls boasted all sorts of treasures. Jewellery, books, art, more books. She lingered at one for a moment then kept walking, reaching for Cameron's hand.

An artist with an easel stood perched at the end of the street. Amelia smiled—he was so quintessentially what she might have imagined a Parisian street artist to look like. Silver hair at the temples, slender, dressed in corduroy trousers with braces over a loose shirt, and a beret on the top of his head, the angle of it charming and jaunty. A family sat before him, their picture being faithfully and quickly mined from the blank page.

'Amelia, look!' Cameron pointed at the portrait, drawing the attention of the little girl in the picture.

'Don't move, Angela,' her mother instructed in a broad American accent. The girl's eyes remained focussed on Cameron, with that curiosity children instinctively have for other children, before she turned back to the artist.

'Can we do one?' Cameron squeezed Amelia's hand, looking up at her and smiling. 'Please?'

Something stuck hard in Amelia's throat. 'Oh, I don't think so.' She bit down on her lip, because even as she issued the refusal a part of her wanted to agree. 'It's late.'

Santos watched, as surprised by his son's suggestion as Amelia evidently was.

'But please,' Cameron insisted. 'So I have a picture of you. For when you…go.' The last word was little more than a whisper, but it screamed through Santos. The pleasure of a moment ago disappeared like a popped balloon.

Amelia's eyes lifted to his and Santos held her gaze, his expression impassive even when his mind was firing. The bond between Cameron and Amelia was unmistakable. It was why he'd insisted she come to Agrios Nisi, and he'd seen evidence of that bond again and again. But hearing Cameron ask for a picture because Amelia was leaving made Santos feel two things: irresponsible, for not properly having appreciated that there was risk in this step—risk that Cameron would become too attached to a temporary part of his life; and excluded, because Cameron's love for Amelia was so apparent. Santos didn't know if their connection was something he'd ever have with his son. He wasn't sure he'd ever have it with anyone.

Amelia had been trying to help him—but that wasn't the answer. Santos had told her that repeatedly. *He* needed to focus on his relationship with Cameron. It was no good to feel excluded from their bond—he had to focus on being the father Cameron deserved. Fear had driven him to employ Amelia—fear of being alone with Cameron, of not being what the little boy needed, but that wasn't acceptable. Santos had never run from a challenge and this was the most important of his life. He would conquer it—he had to.

'What do you say, *monsieur*?' the artist called, taking payment from the mother of the family he'd just drawn and giving his full attention to Santos. 'Let me draw your beautiful family. Your wife and child should be captured on paper, no?'

'Yes,' Cameron agreed with a grin.

'Another time,' Amelia demurred gently then, to Cameron as she guided him away, 'We have plenty of photographs together on my phone. I'll send one to your dad to print.'

Cameron, though, was unusually determined. 'Why can't we get a picture, though? Like that other family before?'

'Because we're not a family.' Santos's words cut through them all, like the shockwave from an earthquake. His eyes met Amelia's and held her startled gaze for a moment before he crouched in front of Cameron. 'You and I are a family, Cameron.' His words were throaty and guttural, filled with an emotion that surprised him with its strength. 'Amelia is just a friend. It's different.'

No one spoke for the rest of the short walk to his apartment. Even Cameron was quiet.

But Amelia's mind had been flooded by his words. *Amelia is just a friend. It's different. We're not a family.*

The silence filled her with a sense that she was drowning.

She felt as if she was on the outside looking in on something incredibly beautiful and warm but being lashed by snow and ice. She was their 'friend', except she wasn't. Her place in both of their lives was temporary.

They were a family. She didn't belong.

The next day, she'd leave. Soon Cameron would start a new school, make new friends and have a different teacher; and, while he might—for a time—think of Miss Ashford, before long she'd be a tiny figment of his imagination, slipping through the recesses of his mind until she was gone for ever. As for Santos?

At the door to the building that housed his penthouse, she looked at him without meaning to, only to find his eyes were resting on her face. Her heart stuttered. Would he think of her when she was gone? Would he miss her?

'Let's go upstairs.'

She nodded her agreement, but her insides were awash with doubts. She hadn't been stupid enough to think saying goodbye would be easy but she'd had no concept of just how damned hard it would turn out to be.

He was used to Paris. Used to the Eiffel Tower, used to the city, used to its sounds and smells, but being here with Amelia on their last night together somehow made it different. New all over again, like the first time he'd come here.

'You were annoyed by him?' Her words reached across the room and he fixed his gaze on her face intently, as if committing it to memory. Maybe he should have let the artist draw the damned picture. He didn't have a photo of himself with Amelia. What a childish thing to care about! Since when had he wanted photographs of his lovers? Boxing her neatly into that shelf filled him with satisfaction. Amelia was no different from anyone else he'd been with. Even as he told himself the comforting fact, he acknowledged it for the lie it was.

'Who?'

She sipped her Scotch, her expression morphing into a grimace as the unfamiliar alcohol assaulted her. 'The artist.'

He searched for the right words. He had been annoyed. Jealous? Excluded? Worried? None of those things particularly did him credit. He focussed on the small part of his response he could claim without a sense of shame. 'I was annoyed for Cameron. He doesn't need to hear that kind of thing—that we're a family when it's patently untrue.'

He shifted his gaze across the room, his eyes landing on the door that led to Cameron's room. They'd left Talia on the island—it was just a short trip, and easy enough for Santos to manage Cameron on his own. Truth be told he was, in some ways, looking forward to being alone with the boy. It was a double-edged sword, though, because that would only happen once Amelia had left.

'It was a natural assumption,' Amelia murmured, but her eyes had fallen away, her expression frustratingly shuttered from his.

'Just as it's natural for Cameron to wish he were part of a family. It's something he's never known— even with his mother. But allowing him to indulge an illusion will only hurt him in the long run. We're not a family and it felt important to explain that to Cameron. Do you disagree?'

It felt good to say the words, as though they were important somehow. Her expression flickered slightly but then she tersely moved her head sideways. Her dark hair was glossy in the evening light. 'No. I...think you were right.' But it was a soft statement, swallowed by swirling emotions. Her concern for Cameron was obvious.

'He'll be fine,' Santos assured her after a quiet moment. 'Don't worry about him.'

'I'll always worry about him,' she said simply, her smile melancholy.

'You don't trust me?'

'I care for him,' she clarified. 'I think loving someone and worrying about them probably go hand in hand.'

He stiffened, her easy use of the word 'love' sparking inside him. She was talking about Cameron, not him, but it nonetheless felt as though danger were surrounding him.

'I was a little...surprised too. I hadn't realised what we would look like, from the outside.' Her smile was awkward. 'It's been a long time since I've had anything even remotely resembling a family.' Her cheeks flushed pink. 'I know we're not. I just meant what people might have thought...'

Her loneliness opened a huge hole in his chest. He tried to cover over it, to ignore it. He'd made a choice to stay single, to avoid emotional commitments, but she hadn't. Not really. Her parents had devastated her, and she'd gone into a mode of self-protection ever since then, but she deserved to be a part of something; she deserved to be loved. The certainty rolled through his gut. She *deserved* to be loved. The idea of that stirred something uncomfortable within him but also brought him a wave of happiness because, more than anything, he wanted her to be happy.

He couldn't make her happy.

Offering her weekend assignations when it suited him would be a bastard's move and she deserved better. Once she left, he'd never see her again; setting her free was the best thing for her.

He resolutely changed the subject. 'Who won your chess game?'

'I did.' Her features relaxed. 'I almost always do, though.'

Santos narrowed his eyes thoughtfully. He had to set her free—and perhaps she wouldn't even mind that much. 'So why do you suppose he continues to play against you?'

'He's a far better player now than he was when we first started competing,' she said simply, taking another drink. This time, her face didn't contort with the hit of alcohol.

'You don't think there could be another reason?'

'Such as?'

'Such as he's attracted to you?'

'Brent?' She pulled a face. 'No way. He's definitely just a friend.'

But Santos wasn't so sure about that. It seemed unlikely and impossible.

'Honestly, there's nothing between us—and never has been.'

'Maybe you should revisit that.'

'Why?'

'He seems nice. You obviously have a lot in common.'

'You don't mean he "seems nice". You mean he's

handsome, and therefore I should feel attracted to him,' she challenged.

'I wouldn't really know what you find handsome,' he responded lightly, drinking his Scotch.

She rolled her eyes. 'I've had very lovely looking men ask me out in the past, thank you very much. That's not what I'm into.'

'You don't like attractive people?'

Her easy smile morphed into a frown of deep concentration. 'The fact you're attractive isn't why I was attracted to you.'

'So why were you?'

He leaned forward, his need to hear her answer surprising him.

'Why after living as a nun or a social isolationist did you decide you wanted me to be your first?'

She stared at her drink so he wanted to reach across and lift her chin, tilting her face towards his, but he didn't. He waited, impatience making his gut clench.

'I can't really say,' she said a little breathlessly. 'I think my stardust and your stardust just aligned.'

It was such a romantic thing for a scientist to say that her expression was self-conscious, and then she laughed. Only to his ears the sound was slightly brittle.

'Sorry. That's a load of nonsense. I bet you can't wait to see the back of me tomorrow.'

CHAPTER TWELVE

'DO YOU HAVE to go?' Pain was lashing Amelia from all directions. The sooner she stood up and walked out of this penthouse, the better.

'I'm afraid so. School starts next week and I have to get the classroom all ready for the new students.'

Tears filled Cameron's eyes. 'I want you to stay here with me.'

Her heart squeezed. She wanted that too, more than she could say. She refused to look at Santos.

Everything was different. Even the way they'd made love the night before had been different. Slower, more explorative, as if they'd both been committing every single detail of each other to memory. It had been a goodbye, an act of passion filled with finality. It was the last time they'd be together.

She'd woken early, slipped from his room, showered and dressed, already mentally imagining herself back in England, in her own home, far from Santos Anastakos and his seductive way of life.

'She can't, Cameron. Miss Ashford was good enough to spend her holidays with you but now it's time for her to leave.'

The coldness in his words was for Cameron's benefit but it only added to the excruciating minefield she was navigating.

'Then I want to go with her.' His little face assumed a truculent expression. 'I want to go home.'

Now she did look at Santos and saw a dark emotion in the depths of his eyes. Neither of them had predicted this. 'You have so much to look forward to, darling. You're going to love your new school, and make so many new little friends.'

'I like my old school and my old friends. I like *you*. I want to go home. I want to go home!' He burst into tears, tears that broke Amelia's heart. He hadn't had an outburst like this in weeks. She wrapped her arms around him, drawing him into a bear hug, holding him right where he was. She wanted to give into a similar breakdown, but didn't. For Cameron, she held it together.

'I'm sorry,' was all she could say, and she meant it from the depths of her heart. She was sorry for all that this little boy had lost. The years he'd missed out on having a father in his life because of a decision his mother had made, then the sudden loss of a mother he'd adored and now the terrifying new start that was before him.

'Do you remember what I told you when we first came to Greece?'

He shook his head, his eyes still overflowing with tears.

'I told you that every night, when you look up in the sky, I'll be looking up at it too. And we'll see the same stars, and we can smile and wave at each other, and you'll know that I'm thinking about you and you're thinking about me. Deal?'

But his lips formed a belligerent frown. 'Please don't go.'

A tear slid out of her eye. She wiped it away discreetly as she stood. 'I have to.' That was firmer, her 'strict teacher' voice. She pressed a hand to his shoulder, squeezing it gently. 'You be a good boy for your daddy, okay?'

Cameron's response was muffled.

Santos crouched down, his eyes at Cameron's height. 'Why don't you go get your shoes on and this afternoon we can go to the very top of the Eiffel Tower?'

'Without Amelia?'

Santos's jaw tightened. 'The view is exceptional. Go and get your shoes.'

Cameron hovered for a moment and then turned on his heel, half-running into his room and slamming the door.

Amelia startled. 'He'll be okay.'

Santos's head jerked in silent agreement and his eyes locked to hers for a moment that filled her with a whole new type of pain. He began to walk towards the door, his stride long. Amelia moved more slowly, aware that every step brought her closer to the end of this.

Everything inside her was pulling, tightening, making her ache in her entire body. Her heart was screaming at her to say something, to suggest they have one more night together, but it was too late for that even if she'd wanted to. She and Santos were consenting adults who'd gone into this with their eyes wide open but Cameron didn't deserve to have his little heart broken any more than it already had been.

They'd agreed this would be the end of it; they had to stick to that.

At the door, she lifted the handle of her suitcase, propping it to her side. 'Leo will take you to the airport.'

'I would have been happy to take the train.'

His smile seemed distracted. Was he already wishing she'd leave? Planning how he'd fill his nights when she was no longer around? The idea activated her pride; she wouldn't let him know how hard she was finding this. 'It's a door-to-door service.' He lifted a hand then, cupping her cheek, running his finger over her lips so she closed her eyes and inhaled, breathing him in. Every fibre of her being was shouting at her to say something. But what?

'Thank you.' Her heart exploded. 'For everything.'

He lifted his other hand, cupping her face. 'I am the one who should thank you, Amelia. I won't forget you.' His eyes were earnest, his voice throaty. She believed him. But that didn't change the fact he'd also replace her swiftly, as was his habit, and never contact her again.

Her stomach rolled; her heart splintered. She had to get out of there. 'Take care of him, okay?'

Their eyes clashed and there was so much in that look, so much unspoken and important. 'I will.' A gravelled admission that exploded through her.

She could barely look at him as she walked away, and every step towards the lift was an agony. The doors opened and she stepped inside, only then trusting her

gaze to flip back to the door of the penthouse, craving
one last look at Santos despite the fact she could see
him with her eyes shut.

The door was closed.

He pressed his back against the door, his breathing
rough, his body tense. Adrenalin hammered through
him.

Go after her.

But what the hell for? Another night? Two? Until he
no longer felt this addictive yearning for her?

He had always had the deepest determination not
to hurt women—women as an abstract concept. With
Amelia, that became very specific.

He wouldn't hurt her. With his life, he pledged that.

Inviting her to stay longer would be a doorway to
pain and he couldn't do it. Already he could see her
ambivalence and uncertainty. She'd been carefully measured but he knew her better than that now.

He had to let her go. He wasn't his father. He didn't
use women for his own selfish purposes, disregard-
ing how that might affect them. Santos was perfectly
capable of having a sexual affair without letting his
emotions into the equation, but he wasn't so sure about
Amelia. The street artist's comment had simply cemented his doubts on that score. She deserved a family—not the illusion of one but the real deal. And, the
longer she spent with Cameron and him, the more likely
she'd be to imagine… He shook his head against the
door, his lungs bursting. It was impossible.

He stayed pressed to the door for several minutes.
Long enough for Amelia's lift to have reached the

lobby, for Leo to have lifted her suitcase into the boot, for him to have pulled the SUV out from the kerb and begun the drive to Charles de Gaulle.

And so she was gone.

He wasn't a fool. The fact he hadn't been with another woman a month after he'd last seen Amelia was an indication of how much their arrangement had affected him.

He wasn't interested in being with anyone else. Not yet. The idea of having sex with any other woman left him cold.

He told himself it was just as well—Cameron wasn't adjusting well to life in Athens and was taking more of Santos's time and attention than he'd anticipated. But, still, his nights were free. Once the six-year-old was in bed, Santos was able to do as he wanted.

And yet he spent his time alone, in his study, catching up on work or losing himself in board reports. He also cursed the day he'd ever met Amelia Ashford.

Teaching made Amelia happy. Winscott Village made Amelia happy. Playing chess with Brent made her happy. Her work on the Hayashi Analysis made her happy.

But in the four weeks since leaving Paris—since leaving Santos and Cameron—Amelia had felt a heaviness deep inside her that nothing was able to shift. There was no happiness in anything any more.

It was a grief—but different from what she'd gone through when her parents had cut her from their life. Those emotions had made sense.

This didn't.

She and Santos had been clear from the start. She'd known all along that she'd be coming back to Winscott to take up her teaching position. She'd known it would end and she'd simply enjoyed the time they had.

So why did she feel as though she was barely holding it together?

The days were something to be got through. She taught, and she went through the motions of being the teacher her pupils needed her to be, but at the end of the day she locked up her classroom and went home, stripping off her clothes as she walked to her bedroom, where she would curl up in bed, pull the duvet to her neck and simply stare at the wall.

The nights were the worst.

She'd outgrown nightmares as a ten-year-old but they were back now. Awful, terrifying nightmares—Cameron running through fire and her not being able to reach him, Santos following behind, neither of them coming out. It was all so vivid that she'd wake up in a sweat and take several seconds to remind herself that it was just a bad dream—they were fine. So far as she knew, at least.

The nights when she didn't have nightmares were even worse, because then her head was filled with Santos—all the ways he'd made himself some sort of master to her body and its impulses; all the ways he'd made her feel more alive than she'd known possible. Those dreams were a form of torture from which she never wanted to wake.

The loneliness was awful.

Having accepted that she was binary within the universe, for the summer she hadn't felt that. She'd felt like she was part of something.

A sob filled her throat. She swallowed it, staring at the wall, squeezing her eyes shut. It was no good. Tears ran down her cheeks. She dashed at them, her heart unbearably heavy, and pulled her knees more tightly to her chest.

She'd *felt* like she was part of something, but she hadn't been. It had been an illusion and Santos had warned her about that right at the very beginning. She'd told him she was capable of separating a physical relationship from anything more.

And can you say with confidence that you will feel that way in five weeks, when you leave the island?

'Oh, God.' She sat up in her bed, brushing her hair from her brow.

She'd done the exact opposite of what she'd promised him. She'd fallen in love with him. It wasn't just sex. Maybe it had never been. Maybe she hadn't just been being trite when she'd said their stardust had aligned.

Santos had been different.

On the first day they'd met, she'd wanted to kiss him so badly. Why? Because he was different and something about him called to her. Generally, her understanding of the world was informed by science, but in this moment she subscribed to every theory she'd ever heard about soul mates and fate.

'I'm in love with Santos.' She pressed her palms into her eyes, shaking her head from side to side in disbelief. And yet there was also a bubbling euphoria, a feeling that almost bordered on the edge of hysteria. She was in love with Santos. Completely. Completely and utterly in love with him. Pushing off the duvet, she stood, a sense of purpose flooding her body for the first time since leaving Paris. Perhaps even sooner than that, for the last week or so of their time together had been tinged with a sense of powerlessness, as though she'd been on a train and couldn't get off.

She loved him.

She had to tell him. Regardless of what he said, she needed him to know. He was scared of hurting her, but was he just letting that fear stop him from having what he really wanted in life? Did he want her like she wanted him?

It was Thursday. The idea of having to get through a whole day at school before the weekend was a unique form of torture, but that same sense of purpose made it possible. She loaded up her phone and began the practicalities, booking flights, organising what she could.

She had to tell him. She'd think about what came next afterwards.

She was sure Cameron would be asleep at eight o'clock on a Friday night, and that was important. As much as she was desperate to see the little boy, she understood how confusing it would be to him, and he deserved better than that. So she'd waited outside his Athens home, her nerves doubling by the minute, her doubts plaguing her, uncertainty ripping through her.

But she knew she had to do this. She needed to tell Santos the truth.

Finally, a minute after eight, she walked up the steps, memories of the last time she'd been here and taken these steps flooding her mind and body. That night had been perfect. If she hadn't loved him before then, she'd definitely fallen hard for him on that evening in Athens.

It was cooler now, autumn wrapping its grip around the country, so she wore jeans, a sweater and a scarf at her throat. Her fingers shook as she lifted them to the door, hesitating for a moment before pressing the buzzer there.

A moment later, it pulled inwards and she braced herself, wondering if it would be Chloe or Leo, perhaps Talia.

It was Santos.

Santos Anastakos, looking so familiar and so different, so untouchably handsome and expensive in a bespoke suit that fit his body like a glove.

'Amelia!' Her name was torn from him, shock evident in all his features.

'Hi.' Her voice was barely a whisper. Inwardly she cursed and tried again. 'How are you?'

He frowned, his eyes shifting beyond her, as if he could somehow understand what she was doing there if he looked hard enough. This wasn't a good start.

Shock though was quickly set aside, his face assuming a distant expression, so he looked at her as though she were a polite stranger. Her stomach dropped to her toes.

'I'm fine. And you?'

As though she meant nothing to him. As though her being here was an inconvenience. Her knees felt weak, like they might not be able to support her for much longer.

She had to do this. She needed to tell him and see where the chips fell.

'Are you going somewhere?'

A frown flashed across his face and he dipped his head forward in silent response. 'Soon.'

Great. A time limit. She toyed with her hands and then stopped, sucking in a deep breath and searching for courage. She loved him and, whatever happened, he deserved to know that. She couldn't live in a world where he *didn't* know how she felt. But the fear of being rejected by him was enormous. She braced for it, straightening her spine, her eyes awash with deep, raw emotions.

'How's Cameron?'

His face tightened, his eyes stormy. 'He's—a work in progress.'

'What does that mean?' For a moment, thoughts of her own misery were driven from her head.

Santos compressed his lips, a muscle throbbing at the base of his jaw. 'Did you come to speak about my son?'

Her heart squeezed. He was being so cold! Her stomach looped in on itself. 'No.' She shook her head, closing her eyes. This was a disaster. But she'd come all this way; she had to do it. Whatever fine beam of hope she'd had when she'd boarded the flight in London was now flickering to darkness inside her.

'But I'd be lying if I said I haven't been thinking about him since I left.' She swallowed. 'And about you.'

The sharp intake of air, signalled by the rising of his chest, was the only indication that her words had any impact on him. His features were blanked of emotion but there was agony in his eyes, a torment that made her heart ache.

'Come in.' It was a command, short and sharp. Hope lifted through her. She looked beyond him but memories flooded her, memories that would eat her alive if she wasn't careful. She shook her head. Whatever he said, being out here felt like a tether to her real world and like a slipstream to escape, if she needed it.

'This won't take long.'

He nodded. Was that relief she saw on his face? Her heart dropped.

'You were so specific, Santos. Right at the start of all this, you were abundantly clear about how you felt and what you wanted. I know that you intended for us—what we were—to be a physical affair that ended when I left.'

His eyes seemed to be tied to hers by some unseen force. He stared at her and she felt as though he were touching her. Butterflies shifted through her belly. Finally, he moved his head, just a tiny mark of agreement. 'We both agreed to that.'

'Yes.' She sighed. 'But it turns out you were right. It's hard to separate emotions from sex. I thought I could do it but, God, Santos…' She shook her head, a dreaded film of tears filling her eyes so she closed them for a second, blinking furiously.

He was tense. She could feel it emanating off him in waves, slamming into her. 'What are you saying?'

'What do you think?' She shook her head and a hysterical laugh bubbled out of her. 'I fell in love with you, just like you said I would.'

His face paled, his jaw tightened. 'Amelia.' He shook his head and then reached for her, putting a hand around her arm. 'No. You can't have.'

Another laugh, completely humourless. 'Well, I did.' She drew in another breath, waiting for it to fill her with some kind of courage. 'And I don't think I'm the only one.'

If it was possible, his face paled even more. 'I was so honest about this.' He groaned, reaching down and squeezing her hand. He took a step out onto the landing, his body closer to hers, as though he wanted to touch her but also knew it would be too complicated. 'This is the last thing I wanted.'

Her throat felt as though it were lined with blades. 'Are you sure about that?'

He ground his teeth. 'Absolutely.' His eyes shuttered closed for a minute. 'I don't love you, Amelia. I'm sorry if I did anything to confuse you, anything to lead you on. I wanted what we shared but I always knew and accepted that it would end.' The words slashed her insides, tearing her to ribbons.

'I don't believe you.' She held his gaze even when her courage was faltering. 'Tell me you haven't thought about me.'

He hesitated for a moment.

'Tell me you haven't missed me.'

He was completely silent.

'Tell me you don't love me.' Her voice cracked but it was so important to hear him say those words.

'If I say those things, it will hurt you, and that is the last thing I want to do. Let me say this instead: I want now what I wanted then. Our relationship ran its course.'

It was, somehow, worse than if he'd just agreed with her. It was an admission that nothing about what they'd shared had affected or changed him at all. Where her heart had been blown wide open, making her not only open to the possibility of love but accepting of its inevitability, he was the same man he'd been before.

She'd come here because she'd thought it was important for him to know how she felt, but now the futility of what she'd set out to do weighed her down more than anything else.

At least before she'd had hope, and she'd had the happiness of her memories—a happiness that might have returned in time.

Now, there was nothing. How could she look back at any of the times they'd been together and not see that what had been an incredibly special moment for her had meant literally nothing to him?

The sound of a taxi door closing had her turning on autopilot and she used the shift as an opportunity to wipe an errant tear from her cheek.

'Santos, darling, I'm so sorry I'm late.' A woman—not Maria but cast from the exact same mould, all leggy, slim, tanned with long blonde hair—stepped from the car and sashayed towards his home on sky-high heels. Her dress was like a second skin, moss-green with a deep V at the front and a slit to mid-thigh.

Amelia spun round to face him, the situation only just making itself obvious to her. What a fool! Here she was pouring her heart out to him and he was waiting on his date! His lover?

She was going to be sick. Oh, God.

She wanted to say something pithy. Something that would make light of this whole affair. She wanted the ground to swallow her whole. But her heart was breaking and she couldn't hide that from him.

The woman came up to them, smiled with curiosity at Amelia then pressed a kiss to Santos's lips. Bile rose in Amelia's throat.

'I don't think we've met.' The woman extended a manicured hand. Amelia stared at it.

'No.' Her voice sounded hollow. She couldn't look at Santos but politeness had her shaking the other woman's slim hand. 'I'm just someone who used to work for Santos.' She swallowed. Tears were engulfing her. She didn't—couldn't—say goodbye. She turned away, gripping the railing for support as she quickly moved down the steps, beyond grateful for her sensible ballet flats. She would never have been able to make a speedy getaway in heels like the other woman's.

The other woman's.

The way she'd leaned in and kissed him… They weren't strangers and this wasn't a first date. The idea of him being with someone else made her ache all over. The taxi was still there, the driver filling something out in his notebook. Amelia tapped on the window as she pulled the passenger door open. But Santos was right behind her, his hand on the door, his body framing hers as she moved to take a seat.

'Wait.' The word was drawn from deep within him, thick and dark. 'Don't go yet.'

A sob bubbled from her throat. 'Why not?' Her eyes lifted to his house. The front door was closed, his glamorous date no doubt ensconced inside.

'You told me all of this. You said I wouldn't matter.

You said you'd never love me. You warned me. You haven't done anything wrong.'

He was so close. She could feel his breath, each one ripped from his body. She had to get out of here. A full-blown breakdown was imminent and she wouldn't subject him to that. She loved him enough not to want him to suffer unnecessary guilt. After all, what had he really done wrong? He'd warned her from the start.

I don't believe in love—not romantic love, in any event. I don't ask you not to love me because I'm arrogant, so much as because it's utterly futile. I will never return it.

He stared at her and she waited for him to speak, but he didn't, and the impossibility of all of this just made it worse. She sank into the taxi, her hand on the door. Still he stood there, his frame blocking the door from closing.

'Please just let me go now.'

He continued to stare at her, his expression dark.

Tears filled her eyes; her heart was breaking. 'I need to go.'

The plaintive cry did it. He seemed to rouse from something and step backward. A second later she pulled the taxi door closed and it drove away, taking her from his home, away from a scene that would be etched in the fibres of her being for ever.

CHAPTER THIRTEEN

EVERY MORNING FOR the next week, he woke with a feeling of weight bearing down on him, suffocating him. Every day for the next week, he struggled to so much as breathe.

When he slept, he saw Amelia. Her eyes, her smile, her frown, her pain. The moment Pia had arrived and Amelia had seen her, he'd wanted to throttle something, or to reach out and stop time, to undo what had just happened.

How could she fail to believe he was sleeping with Pia? And then Pia had kissed him and stood at his side, as though they were a duo and Amelia a stranger, and he'd been incapable of doing anything but standing there, so blindsided by what she'd said, by the heart she was offering him, that he'd been temporarily immobilised.

It hadn't been good enough. Amelia had looked at Pia and believed that he was already seeing other women. Hell, hadn't that been his plan? Hadn't he thought that taking Pia to the fundraiser ball—an event for which he was on the board—might lead to him feeling something for her? And he would have been relieved if that had been the case. If finally he could have looked at another woman and felt even the slightest flare of interest.

Amelia couldn't have known that he'd been celibate since Paris. Amelia couldn't have known that the idea of so much as having dinner with another woman disgusted him. How could he sit across the table from someone else and make small talk when anyone else now bored him senseless?

His father's announcement—that he was getting divorced again—only added to the weight pressing on Santos's chest. All these people and their damned belief in 'love'. It destroyed lives. Look at Amelia and how she was feeling! She'd let herself fall in love with him and now she was suffering.

He focussed on two aspects of his life to the exclusion of all else: Cameron and his work.

But, two weeks after Amelia had turned up on his doorstep, Cameron came home from school with a torn shirt pocket.

'What happened?' Santos reached out and ran his finger over it, something in the little boy's demeanour instinctively leading him to understand the seriousness of this.

'Nothing.' Cameron crossed his arms over his chest. 'I don't want to talk about it.'

'Cameron?' Santos's voice was unintentionally sharp. He softened it with effort. 'I cannot help you if I don't know—'

'Just leave me alone.' Cameron burst into tears and stormed down the corridor, slamming his bedroom door shut.

Great.

He listened to the little boy's sobbing and pressed his head against the wall. Everything was falling apart. A year ago his life had been ordered and neat. He'd been absorbed by his work, his commercial success a blinding light, and he'd enjoyed his social life too—sex, friendships; easy. He'd been *happy*.

He pushed up from the wall a little, his chest straining. No, he hadn't been happy. He'd been existing. The only time he'd ever really been happy was on the island, over the summer. That beautiful, enormous mansion that was his connection to his heritage, a place where he was most at home, had suddenly felt like a *real* home. Returning each evening to Amelia and Cameron had become what he'd lived for. Knowing that within minutes of his helicopter touching down he would see Amelia, that he would be able to steal a kiss when Cameron wasn't looking.

His stomach clenched. Her smile had become the most important thing in his life. But she wasn't smiling now. She was miserable, and all because she'd fallen in love with him.

Just like the women who'd loved his father.

Pain was the inevitable cost of love. How could she fail to see that? Why hadn't she protected herself better? Even her own parents had failed her, so why the hell had she put her faith in him? How could she have thought loving him was a smart idea?

Because she couldn't help it; a voice in his head demanded to be heard. *Love isn't like that.*

He listened to Cameron's sobs subsiding a little, and then went into the kitchen, pulling out a box of ice-creams and opening one. Even that filled him with memories.

Maybe if he'd been stricter from the start, enforced tighter caps on what they were, rationed Amelia to being a 'sometimes' lover... Perhaps if he'd come home later, made sure that while they'd been sleeping together they weren't also dining together, working side by side, doing all the things that might in different circumstances have characterised a real family...

He felt like he'd been punched in the chest. He didn't *want* a real family. But he did want Amelia. He wanted her in his life, smiling, happy, pursuing her dreams but at his side.

But then what? another voice niggled at him. What if in a year's time they wound up in this exact same position? What if he was even more like his father than he realised? What if he promised her the world and then changed his mind?

He knocked on Cameron's door.

'Go away.'

'I have ice-cream.'

A pause. A sob. Then the door handle opened to reveal his son's tear-stained face. Santos felt an anguish unlike anything he'd ever known. He wanted Amelia on a lot of levels but there was this, too. With her at his side, everything made sense, and he knew he was a better parent with her support. It was only a small part of why he needed her, but it was the straw that had broken the camel's back.

He wanted her, but this time he'd be more careful. He'd protect her better. What he needed was a contract, a document that spelled everything out in black and white, a way of ensuring she wouldn't get hurt this time around.

* * *

This had been a mistake. Amelia was a scientist first and a teacher next. She was, as it turned out, definitely not a cook. She stared at the front of her apron, covered in a pale yellow goo, and turned the tap on with her elbow. Water spurted out too hard, splashing her face. She ground her teeth together and eased the tap off, pushing her hands beneath the stream then adding some soap and lathering them up.

'Make pasta, they said. It will be easy, they said.' She cast an eye over the tragedy of her chopping board. Whatever the heck she'd assembled, it more closely resembled some kind of blobby sea creature than it did anything edible.

When her hands were clean, she moved back to the chopping board—the mess wasn't contained to one patch of timber, though. It had spread over the kitchen bench. Flour, broken eggs, a rolling pin that would probably never look the same. The television chef with his cockney accent and roguish smile had made it look so easy.

He'd lied.

It wasn't easy.

Grimacing, she lifted the chopping board, preparing to throw the evidence of her failure away, when the doorbell sounded. Casting a glance at the clock, she replaced the board and wiped her hands on the sides of the apron, making sure they were dry.

The supplies she'd ordered for her pupils were already two days later than expected. That had to be them. She moved through her home, not stopping to check her appearance in the mirror—she knew she must look a mess, with flour on her cheeks and in her hair, wearing a sloppy jumper and loose-fitting jeans, but what did she care?

She pulled the door inwards, preparing to sign the postal form and take the box of stationery, except it wasn't Russell, the familiar Royal Mail delivery guy.

'Santos?' Everything inside her began to quiver. The cells of her body went into overdrive. With an enormous effort, she assumed a mask of cool civility, but it was almost impossible when she felt as if she were being electrocuted.

'Amelia.' His brow crinkled and his eyes swept over her, the corner of his lips pulling into a small smile. 'What the hell have you been doing?'

Oh, God. She must look…terrible. But so what? She refused to care about that. Tilting her chin, she held his eyes. 'I'm cooking.'

'Really?'

It was a joke. She ignored it. Her body was buzzing and humming and her chest was compressing. 'What are you doing here?'

He sobered, nodding, shoving his hands in his pocket. 'I came to see you.'

She bit down on her lip. 'Is something wrong?'

'No. Yes.' He stared at her, then expelled a breath. 'Can I come in?'

She looked over her shoulder, then turned back to him. 'I…okay. Just for a minute.'

'Thank you.' She stepped back, giving him plenty of space to move by without touching her, but it still wasn't enough. His hand brushed hers and she almost jumped out of her skin. She covered her response by pushing the door shut with a resounding click. From there, she kept her distance, maintaining at least a metre of space between them when they reached the living room.

He looked around, his eyes taking in all the details, so she tried to see it as he must—the homeliness of it, the simplicity and cosiness. It was completely different from his perfectly designed living spaces.

She squared her shoulders, assuming a position of defiance and defensiveness rather than showing how affected she was by his presence.

'*Christos.*' He shook his head, then dragged a hand through his hair. 'I have no idea what to say to you.'

How could he not hear her heart? It was slamming into her ribs over and over, so loud, so painfully persistent.

'Then why are you here?'

'Let me start with this.' He nodded decisively, moving towards the window and looking out at the empty field that ran beyond her house, all the way to the stream. 'When you came to Athens, I was going to a fundraising event. I'm on the board and obliged to attend. It wasn't a date.'

And, despite the fact he wasn't looking at her, she turned away from him, staring at a photograph on the wall.

'I didn't sleep with her. Or anyone else. I haven't moved on from you, Amelia.'

She kept staring at the photo, his words wrapping around her, making her heart hurt, her breath burn, her body sag.

'I wanted to, though. That night, I thought that if I

could just do something I normally would that maybe I would start to *feel* normal again. Maybe if I went out with someone like Pia, laughed with her, flirted with her, you wouldn't take up such a huge part of my mind any more. I needed to perform an exorcism, and I thought that would work.'

Amelia spun round to face him, hurt showing on her features, her eyes huge in her face. 'I don't know if that's more offensive to her or to me. You thought that you could sleep with her and forget about me? You'd actually use another woman like that?'

He blanched. 'I thought I'd feel *something* for her. Desire. Need. Anything. But I haven't felt a damned thing since you left. Why is that?' he asked, crossing his arms over his chest. 'How come you're all I can think about? How come you're the only person I want, the only person I need?'

She clamped her mouth shut, her head issuing a stern warning to her heart. None of this meant anything. He was annoyed by her hold on him, but hadn't that been the case all along? He'd been transfixed by her and waiting for that to wear off. He hadn't wanted to feel that way; he didn't welcome any of this.

He was moving closer to her and, while she braced for his nearness, there was a tiny part of her that wanted to welcome him. That wanted to run towards him and beg him to stay a just bit longer. She hated that part of herself. Speaking of exorcisms...

'How come waking up without you makes me feel like I'm missing a part of myself? How come you're the last person I want to see before I fall asleep at night?' He moved closer, his body almost touching hers now.

She made a small noise, a choking sound. Of fear? Or of want?

'How come everything feels dull and pointless without you? How come I look for you all the time? How come I miss you so much I can barely breathe?' Another step and his body pressed to hers, his hand lifting to cup her cheek.

'How come I have told myself all my life that I would never be like my father, that I would never let a woman fall in love with me, and I sure as hell wouldn't ever love a woman, and yet I love you?'

She drew in a deep gulp of air, shaking her head and stepping backwards. 'Don't.' It took all her willpower and strength to separate from him. 'Don't come here now and say this. Don't you dare.'

'I fell in love with you, Amelia. It is the opposite of what I thought I wanted but here I am, a broken man, an incomplete man, without you in my life. Your love has become the sum total of what I want. What choice do I have *but* to come here and say this to you?'

'You hurt me.' He winced as though she'd hit him. 'You did exactly what you've spent your whole life telling yourself you wouldn't, and you hate yourself for that, so you're trying to fix it. You can't just say you love me! That's not the answer to this.'

He shook his head, moving closer again, his body wrapping hers inwards, his arms linking behind her back. 'I'm not just saying this to make myself feel better. Yes, I hurt you.' He dropped his forehead to hers. 'I hurt you and seeing that pain on your face is an image I will never forget. When you looked at Pia, when she kissed me, the look in your eyes…' He shook his head, the sentence unfinished.

Pain was burning her insides anew. 'Please don't.'

'But your hurt was matched by my own. I have been miserable without you, and all I can think about is the rest of my life, spending it like this, and there's just this huge, dark void. Without you, nothing has meaning. You are my everything, Amelia.'

She sobbed, her eyes pleading when they met his. 'Please don't say these things.'

'Do you love me?'

She swept her eyes shut, her lips parted. 'Of course.'

'Then why can't I say this? Why can't I say it back to you?'

She sobbed and shook her head. 'Because I know what you want in life and it's not this. You shouldn't have to change who you are because of me.'

'You changed who I am and what I want. Until I met you, of course I felt that love was a fantasy, a ridiculous construct. Until I met you, I'd never been in love before. You taught me to love—I love you, I love Cameron; you opened my heart. I'm still terrified of hurting you, or not being the father he needs, but you showed me that loving someone isn't about not feeling afraid, it's just about showing up and doing your best. Being there for the person you love. All I want in this life is you, Amelia.'

He brushed his lips to hers and she felt as though she were being breathed back to life. Her heart began to sing. 'That artist in Paris saw something I was too stupid to recognise. Or maybe I recognised it and was just too stubborn to accept it. We *are* a family—you, me and Cam—and we should be together.'

Her heart was soaring inside her. 'I can't believe this.'

He compressed his lips and nodded, lifting a hand and padding his thumb over her lower lip, his eyes following the movement before he dropped his hand and stepped away. 'I've given it a lot of thought. I hurt you and I would be a fool to expect you to simply forgive and forget. I know I need to prove myself to you again, and I'm prepared to do that. Here's what I want.' And suddenly, he was the self-made billionaire tycoon success story all over again. Powerful, commanding, completely in his element.

'The school year has just started—I know you won't want to leave your students midway through. And Cameron has just started his new school and, while it's not exactly working out as I'd hoped, I don't believe in giving up, so I think it's important he persevere a little longer.'

Her heart skidded to a stop. 'What do you mean, it's not working?'

'It's a long story.'

'Is he not happy?'

'No, he's not happy. And, while I think he's struggling with the school and his peers, and the differences of culture and language, ultimately I think he misses you more than he—at six—can put into words.'

Her heart cracked open. Tears ran down her cheeks. 'I miss him too.'

A muscle jerked in Santos's jaw. 'Give me the rest of the school year.' It was a command but she heard the uncertainty and doubt, as though he was worried she would refuse him. 'You can fly to Athens on week-ends and I'll come here as often as I can leave Cameron. You can see for yourself how serious I am before you agree to this.'

'Agree to what?'

He stared at her blankly. 'To marry me, obviously.'

She stared back, just as blankly. 'To marry you? Santos, you don't believe in marriage.'

'I don't believe in my father's marriages, but I believe in anything you and I do together.'

A tremble ran down her spine. He blinked, as if just remembering something, turning towards the sofa and picking up a slim leather document wallet. She hadn't even realised he'd been carrying it when he walked in.

'To that end, I've had this drawn up.' He pulled out some paper and handed it to her. His eyes were boring into her so it was hard to concentrate as she skimmed the words.

'A pre-nuptial agreement?' Her heart sped up. 'You've had a pre-nup drawn up? I haven't even agreed—'

'I wanted you to see it before you did agree,' he said quietly, the words earnest and husky.

'*If* I were to marry you, it wouldn't be for the money. Do you honestly think you need to protect your fortune from me?'

'Read it.'

She glared at him then flicked the front page. Then the next. It was all standard legalese until she reached the division of assets list on page three.

'This says that if we got divorced you'd pay out ninety per cent of your shares in Anastakos Inc. to me.' She kept reading. 'And give me the island?' Her eyes lifted to his, her skin paling.

'Keep reading.'

She swallowed and turned the page. 'You'd give me shared custody of Cameron.'

'If you agree to marry me, you'll be his stepmother. I would never ask you to love my son as your own without affording you genuine parental rights. Including custody. I know you love him, Amelia, and he loves you. We're family.'

'Santos.' She shoved the papers at him as though she'd been burned. 'Stop.'

He shook his head. 'I need you to understand that I've thought all this through. I'm not just offering to marry you on a whim. I'm prepared to go all in with this.'

'I think you're missing the point of a pre-nuptial agreement. They're intended to *protect* your fortune.'

'This one is to protect you.'

She shook her head, none of this making any sense. 'So you end up married to me for a lifetime because you can't afford to divorce me? Santos, no. Marriage shouldn't be about money. It's a leap of faith two people take together. Just loving you is enough for me—that's enough to show me that I can trust our future. A pre-nuptial agreement that prepares for divorce? It makes me think you're still just as afraid as ever.'

'Afraid? I'm terrified. I'm terrified of hurting you, and I'm terrified of failing you, but my God, Amelia, what I am most afraid of is living my life without you. If I walk out of this lovely little cottage without knowing that I have made you understand how much I love you? That scares me more than I can say.'

She lifted her eyes to the ceiling, tears filling her lashes.

'This pre-nuptial agreement is not because I don't trust our future. It's because I do trust it. I want to marry you, and I do not believe, for even one moment, that our marriage will fail. I am willing to bet everything I own, everything I am, on that because, as far as I can tell, there's no way I can lose.'

Her eyes widened and she glanced at him, his words weaving through her, making her smile for the first time since leaving Paris.

'You really love me?'

'Oh, yes, *agape*, with every single fibre of my heart, and I always will.'

It was the longest year of Santos's life, but it was what he'd promised Amelia and he had no intention of breaking that promise. He understood how important it was for her to finish her teaching year, but a few months after they'd agreed to marry all he wanted was to have his family together under one roof. His fiancée, his son, the rest of their lives ahead of them.

It was the right decision to wait, though. Cameron settled into a routine at school and had made some good friends. While Santos hadn't doubted the strength of his love for even a moment, he was glad for Amelia's sake that they'd waited a year because proving himself to her was hugely important.

Their wedding was small, just as they'd both wanted. Just a few friends, including Brent, some teachers from

Elesmore, some of his closest friends, his half-brother and father. They'd married at Damen's restaurant, the view of Athens glowing beneath them, and then they'd flown to the island, just the two of them, to start their married life in the very place his life had really started. It was only in meeting Amelia that he'd truly become whole.

On their first night as a married couple, Amelia lay with her head on Santos's arm on a blanket spread across the beach, the sand beneath them, the water lapping close to their toes, looking up at the sky. Stars sparkled and the ancient beauty of the sky seemed to congratulate them. Of all the stardust in all the world, they'd found each other, and their happiness was perfect and for eternity.

* * * * *

If you found yourself head over heels for
Hired by the Impossible Greek,
you'll love these other stories
by Clare Connelly!

The Greek's Billion-Dollar Baby
Bride Behind the Billion-Dollar Veil
Redemption of the Untamed Italian
The Secret Kept from the King

Available now!

#3837 THE PRICE OF A DANGEROUS PASSION
by Jane Porter
Charlotte already broke her biggest rule by giving in to temptation with former client Brando. But a marriage of duty for their baby's sake? No, thank you. Unless Brando can break his own number one rule: keeping his heart off-limits.

#3838 PROMOTED TO HIS PRINCESS
The Royal House of Axios
by Jackie Ashenden
Calista is an elite soldier trained to win any battle. But what happens when the fight is within? Resisting the charismatic prince she's protecting is getting harder by the minute. When his shirt comes off, so do her inhibitions...

#3839 THE TERMS OF THE SICILIAN'S MARRIAGE
The Sicilian Marriage Pact
by Louise Fuller
After just one earth-shattering encounter, Imma is stunned when Vicenzu proposes! Until she learns his motives... If Vicenzu seeks vengeance against her family from their union, she wants freedom. So begins the most passionate of negotiations...

#3840 CLAIMING HIS OUT-OF-BOUNDS BRIDE
by Annie West
When Olivia Jennings is jilted days before her elaborately planned wedding, Alessandro Sartori offers himself as groom. Their families will get the merger they want. And he'll finally get the bride he craves...

YOU CAN FIND MORE INFORMATION ON UPCOMING HARLEQUIN TITLES, FREE EXCERPTS AND MORE AT HARLEQUIN.COM.

HPCNMRB0720

*Dante has no doubt Mia is off-limits. Yet the sparks
between them are an inferno waiting to erupt. And erupt
it does, into an unforgettable encounter that leaves Dante
stunned by Mia's innocence…and his craving for more!*

*Read on for a sneak preview of
Carol Marinelli's next story for Harlequin Presents,*
Italy's Most Scandalous Virgin.

Dante's want for her was perpetual, a lit fuse he was constantly stamping out, but it was getting harder and harder to keep it up. His breathing was ragged; there was a shift in the air and he desperately fought to throw gas on the argument, for his resistance was fast fading. "What did you think, Mia, that we were going to walk into the church together? A family united? Don't make me laugh…"

No one was laughing.

"Take your tea and go to bed." Dante dismissed her with an angry wave of his hand, but even as he did so he halted, for it was not his place to send her to bed. "I didn't mean that. Do what you will. I will leave."

"It's fine. I'm going up." She retrieved the tray.

"We leave tomorrow at eleven," he said again as they headed through to the entrance.

"Yes."

She turned then and gave him a tight smile, and his black eyes meet hers, and there was that look again between them, the one they had shared at the dining table. It was a look that she dared not decipher.

His lips, which were usually plump and red, the only splash of color in his black-and-white features, were for once pale. There was a muscle leaping in his cheek, and she was almost sure it was pure contempt, except her body was misreading it as something else.

She had always been aware of his potent sexuality, but now Mia was suddenly aware of her own.

Conscious that she was naked beneath the gown, her breasts full and heavy, she was aware of the lust that danced inappropriately in the air between them. The prison gates were parting further and she was terrified to step out.

"Goodnight," she croaked, and climbed the stairs, almost tipping the tray, only able to breathe when she heard the door slam.

Tea forgotten, she lay on the bed, frantic and unsettled. So much for the Ice Queen! She was burning for him in a way she had never known until she'd met Dante.

Mia had thought for a long time that there was something wrong with her, something missing in her makeup, for she'd had little to no interest in sex. Even back at school she would listen in on her peers, quietly bemused by their obsessive talking about boys and the things they did that to Mia sounded filthy. Her mother's awkward talk about the facts of life had left Mia revolted. The fact of Mia's life: it was something she didn't want! There was no reason she could find. There had been no trauma, nothing she could pin it to. Just for her, those feelings simply did not exist. Mia had tried to ignite the absent fire and had been on a couple of dates, but had found she couldn't even tolerate kisses, and tongues positively revolted her. She couldn't bear to consider anything else.

And while this marriage had given her a unique chance to heal from the appalling disaster that had befallen her family, the deeper truth was that it had given her a chance to hide from something she perhaps ought to address.

A no-sex marriage had felt like a blessing when she and Rafael had agreed to it.

Yet the ink had barely dried on the contract when she had found out that though those feelings might be buried deep, they were there after all.

Mia had been just a few days into the pretend position of Rafael's PA, and the carefully engineered rumors had just started to fly, when Dante Romano had walked in. A mere moment with him had helped her understand all she had been missing, for with just a look she found herself reacting in a way she never had before.

His dark eyes had transfixed her, the deep growl of his voice had elicited a shiver low in her stomach, and even his scent, as it reached her, went straight to form a perfect memory. When Dante had asked who she was, his voice and his presence had alerted, startled and awoken her. So much so that she had half expected him to snap his fingers like a genie right before her scalding face.

Three wishes?

You.

You.

You.

Don't miss
Italy's Most Scandalous Virgin,
available August 2020 wherever
Harlequin Presents books and ebooks are sold.

Harlequin.com